October 2008

To Lisa:

It's fun to remember our
happy days at K.H.S.

Jeannine Dahlberg

Evil Web of Deceit

by
Jeannine Dahlberg

authorHOUSE®

AuthorHouse™
1663 Liberty Drive, Suite 200
Bloomington, IN 47403
www.authorhouse.com
Phone: 1-800-839-8640

First published by AuthorHouse 8/29/2008

ISBN: 978-1-4389-0304-0 (sc)

Library of Congress Control Number: 2008906306

Printed in the United States of America
Bloomington, Indiana

This book is printed on acid-free paper.

To my daughters Heidi and Erika who encourage me to write my stories.

And

To my eight grandchildren with whom, together, we create our own fairytales.

And

To my brother Fred, whose knowledge never ceases to amaze me.

Chapter One

Thunderheads gathered in the sky all afternoon and into the evening hours confirming a weather report that heavy rain was expected in the area. The prospect of a severe thunderstorm, however, did not deter guests from arriving for one of the most glamorous, prestigious social events of the season at Mason Manor.

Inside, Martin Mason, a well-dressed distinguished gentleman, paced the floor in his study anxiously awaiting the arrival of a frequent visitor. He was outwardly nervous, running his fingers through his thinning grey hair and constantly glancing toward a partially opened window. He was no longer in good health, and the prime of his life had passed long ago. As a younger man, the length of time was of no consequence when manipulating large financial transactions to a profitable fruition, but now, patience was no longer his one and only redeeming virtue. At his advanced age, he lacked the physical stamina to endure the mental, tactical games played in the constant struggle for power within his organization -- games that tested his ruthless, clever ingenuity, which often included opening a bag of dirty tricks.

Martin continued pacing the floor with shoulders pulled back and stretching tall, trying to emanate a much younger man while bracing for the forthcoming meeting. He was determined to end the blackmail, tonight. He had made arrangements earlier in the week to dispose of this nuisance that was festering like a huge ugly boil.

His plan was to have the blackmailer killed at the window, making it appear as if the blackmailer had forced entry into the study.

The tick-tock of the beautifully carved wall clock seemed to get louder with each passing moment and was in concert with the rhythmic beat of his heart. His anxiety raced to a feverish pitch when his thoughts conjured up the many ugly scenes and the constant bickering among his three children for control of his extensive financial empire. Martin's last fatherly talk with each of his children did not go very well, and since their meeting, no one has breached the silence to make amends. He spun around, made an abrupt halt, pounded his fist on the desktop and vowed he would deal with his children in the morning. He wanted it all to end, now!

He reflected in deeper thought upon those earlier hectic years when business constraints constantly pulled him away from his first wife and children. With firm conviction, he silently made a second vow that he would live out his golden years with his new bride in a blissful marriage.

The door to the study opened quickly, breaking his concentration. Startled, he turned around to see his bride of four months standing in the doorway. With a feeling of lust and pride, he stood looking at his young wife. He enjoyed comparing her beauty to the ancient zaftig Greek goddess Venus de Milo, albeit his bride is quite slender. For a brief moment, his fearful anxiety for the impending meeting at the window subsided. A powerfully sexual desire rippled through his body as he gazed tenderly at his wife with eyes that openly conveyed genuine love. He passionately kissed her soft lips and continued to hold her tightly in his arms for a few moments, enjoying the warmth of her body close to his. He knew he was a lucky man. He gently released his embrace and whispered in her ear that she should greet the guests without him. His excuse was he wanted to put some papers away that were lying on his desk before joining the party.

Martin stood in the doorway for a few moments watching his wife's graceful, curvaceous figure move slowly down the hall. She is beautifully dressed in an expensive celadon-green silk gown, which compliments her long auburn hair and hazel-green eyes. He watched as her slender hips swayed to the sound of music coming from the atrium area. It did not bother him when some of his rough-hewn friends both chided and teased him with proverbial slurs and jokes about his "trophy wife". Martin was impervious to all comments, which were made in a cold, cruel, calculating manner. The thought only made him strut more like a peacock that he should be so lucky as to win such a beautiful young woman at his advanced age. He closed the door to his study to the sound of laughter from the guests echoing through the hallway. He continued to pace in the dimly lit study with only brief lightning strikes close by occasionally illuminating the austere atmosphere of the room. Time seemed to stand still as rain continued to pelt the window... and he thought: I'll be glad when this night is over. Let this be the last of it.

The clock chimed the appointed hour when there was a quiet peck on the windowpane. Martin opened the window half way to allow the blackmailer to poke his head and shoulders partially through the window to escape the rain while they talked. The encounter was brief and the two quietly whispered in agitated tones for a short while. Martin became enraged and forcibly grabbed and partially pulled the figure through the open window while snorting expletives and the two wrestled at the window exchanging brutal punches. In the heat of the fight, Martin tried to scan the tree-lined area of the yard looking for his hired assassin... but saw no one. In total frustration, Martin fiercely shoved the figure from the window into the wet bushes; and with a hurried push on the window, partially closed it. Had his plan gone sour? His eyes danced with a renewed glimmer of hope when a flash of lightning revealed the assassin a short distance away. Martin turned from the window to sit at the desk to regain his composure and to await the immediate, prearranged sound of a gunshot... then Martin slumped forward scattering the newspaper clippings before him while a pool of blood quickly grew at his head. The unexpected had happened.

A single gunshot muffled by a strategically awaited clap of thunder had disturbed no one in the adjacent rooms. Houselights streamed through the large windowpanes of the french doors onto the beautifully manicured grounds, which surrounded the mansion illuminating the silhouettes of two lone figures swiftly and silently moving away from the house. A torrent of rain rapidly pounded the dirt into mud removing any semblance of footprints beneath the window. Guests at the charity auction/dinner party were unaware their host Martin Mason was dead.

Chapter Two

Mason Manor is located a good twelve miles north of Spring Grove nestled in the foothills of the Ozark Mountains overlooking the Cedar Valley River.   Usually, Darren Doyle, a private investigator, enjoyed the scenic ride north out of town on Highway 8, but this evening was different. The rapid staccato beat of rain on the car windshield and the pulsating motion of the windshield wipers produced an extra precautionary sense to remain alert while steering the car on the dark winding road. Finally, he reached the entrance gate where he was met by a police officer who looked quite disgruntled standing in the rain. Spotlights from parked police cars swept the grounds around the house creating an eerie atmosphere of strobe lighting bouncing off the rain.

Darren arrived at the mansion to a familiar sight of the usual entourage of forensic staff, medical examiner, paramedics and cops who were already at the crime scene. Television cameras were grinding away on the verandah while rain continued to drench the area; and media personnel pushed and shoved one another to obtain the best angle for conducting an interview with anyone knowledgeable of the details of the investigation. No media personnel were allowed inside the mansion while the police interrogated each guest privately and then escorted each one out the back door for discretionary purposes. The guest list read like "who's who" and no one wanted to be identified or singled out in the morning headlines splashed across the papers announcing the murder of Spring Grove's wealthiest citizen.

This was Darren's second visit to Mason Manor in the past two months. The first call came from Mrs. Mason when she summoned him to investigate a robbery at the manor. As she explained, she believed a private investigator could handle the minor incident more quietly than involving the police department. Martin Mason believed the robbery to be inconsequential since the only room that had been disturbed was his study and nothing of any real value was taken -- just some old newspaper clippings. Darren asked the usual questions, but he knew without the full cooperation of the Masons, nothing would come from the investigation and he wondered why Mrs. Mason even bothered to call him.

He made a thorough mental note of the large study. Expensive sculptured figures were placed decoratively in the room and a few impressionistic oil paintings hung on the walls embracing a room filled with beautifully appointed furniture. Even the office accouterments placed on the desk were richly ornamented. Darren surmised Mr. Mason was an art collector with impeccable taste and it was evident he had the money to support his expensive hobbies. He wondered why the intruder would take only newspaper clippings. There was no forced entry, but he noticed the window behind the desk was partially open, presumably to let some fresh air into the study. The room was neat and tidy and did not give the appearance of having been ransacked. With nothing more to be said or done, Darren left the home with a hurried good-bye from the Masons. He had mixed vibes about pursuing the investigation, and he soon forgot the incident after receiving an envelope containing a rather curt note from Mrs. Mason stating his services were no longer required. More impressively, there was a large check enclosed for an hour's work, which soothed his frustration... but that was two months ago.

This second visit to Mason Manor is quite different. Mrs. Mason excused herself from her guests, who were detained by the police in the atrium, and called to the policeman at the door to escort Darren into the study. The police officer flashed him an unfriendly, silly smirk as if he were tolerating his presence and beckoned Darren to follow him, while policemen continued to scurry back and forth in the hallway conducting their routine investigation. Darren could feel the old animosity building again between him and the police department. Being the son of the mayor of Spring Grove proved to be more of a hindrance than a benefit.

Darren slowly scrutinized the room trying to envision the scene that transpired prior to Martin's death. He walked behind the desk to view the immediate ground and bushes outside beneath the window. But with the torrential rainfall, he knew all evidence of someone's lurking outside the window would have been immediately washed away. He pondered at great length the importance of Mason's jacket sleeves soaked with rain while the front and back of his jacket were dry. Most disturbing, was the same partially opened window, as he had noticed at the time of his first investigation at Mason Manor.

Mrs. Mason lingered awhile in the powder room primping before entering the crowded hallway for the long walk to the study for her private meeting with Darren. She opened the door to the study and in a loud, but quavering voice announced for all to hear, "I told Martin to let it go, but he wanted to be rid of the problem. He wouldn't listen... and now he is dead."

The policemen in the hallway quickly looked at one another hoping to hear more, as she wiped the tears from her eyes with trembling hands and closed the door behind her. To gain her composure, she stood for a few seconds with her back against the closed door.

Darren could not believe his eyes as he watched her swagger across the room and stop within inches of him. He thought: *What have I just witnessed? What a transformation! This is now a woman who is in complete control.* Her body language, as she stood close to him, and her haughty demeanor did not bode well. For a young bride of four months, she showed no visible signs of grief. While her long hair softened her physical beauty, it was the cold calculating look in her eyes that betrayed there was no compassion or sensual feelings for her husband's murder. Darren surmised, as he had heard, she was Martin Mason's trophy wife and his instantaneous dislike for her sparked a premonition of impending distrust.

7

The two stood beside the desk looking at Martin Mason's dead body, which was slumped in the chair with his head and arms resting on the desk. Water drained from Martin's wet tuxedo jacket sleeves and mixed with the blood from his head wound, obliterating everything written on the papers strewn across the desk. Darren was totally baffled that only his sleeves were wet and wondered how this could have happened. Rain continued pelting the window; and with the exception of small glass fragments on the floor caused by the bullet penetrating the windowpane, nothing in the room appeared to be disturbed.

Mrs. Mason was the first to break the silence, and with a strong sense of conviction stated, "I must talk to you, but not here... not today. I am going to insist the will be read as quickly as possible after the funeral and I want you to be present. Then we will talk." She quietly opened the door and quickly glanced down the hallway to see that no one was watching her. With a strong tug on Darren's coat sleeve, she pressed seductively closer, whispering in his ear, "Let's hope we can solve Martin's murder, quickly."

Darren watched Mrs. Mason slowly meander down the hallway visibly shaking with grief while wiping the tears from her eyes, as the policemen offered their condolences. He rubbed the back of his neck thinking, *what a master of deception. She's as good at it as my dad.* He rolled his eyes with a quizzical smirk on his lips. *Was she coming on to me? Her husband's body isn't even cold, yet.*

Darren was confronted at the door by the police lieutenant who made it quite clear that he was not allowed to conduct his own search of the mansion or to talk to any of the guests until after the police had concluded their investigation. Darren said nothing; gave a nonchalant shrug of the shoulders, and headed for the front door.

Chapter Three

The drive to Spring Grove's city hall is a relatively short distance from Darren's apartment, but it may just as well be a trip to another planet. He always feels the weight of the world is on his shoulders when he visits his dad, who has been mayor of Spring Grove for seven years and who is totally absorbed in playing the dutiful politician. He hates their little chats.

Darren parked the car in front of the city hall and walked slowly up the stairs to the door. He was in no hurry as a rash of irritating thoughts rushed through his mind. How many times has he heard his dad say: *It is my pleasure to serve my constituents in helping to make Spring Grove a premiere city.* It all sounds so honorable, but Darren knows it is the power and celebrity status that his dad enjoys. Serving has never been one of his dad's redeeming virtues.

At home, his dad rules like a dictator with no quarter given. Compassion and forgiveness are virtues, which elude him, believing they are signs of weakness. Darren has little respect for him -- both as a father and as a politician.

The family core started to crumble years ago when both his sister Margo and his brother Matt moved out of the house immediately after college and never bothered to keep in touch. Only Darren lives in Spring Grove, now, and he alone has to take the brunt of his dad's caustic diatribe when he sounds off in a tirade of profanities always berating him for choosing to be a private detective.

Perhaps, if Darren had become a contender in the political arena, as his father had wanted, closer ties could have been established between father and son. His father, however, certainly is not a pillar of virtue making him a poor model to follow. In fact, Darren worried that he would inherit his father's traits, which thought was too scary, as he definitely did not want to be like his father.

Mayor Doyle works diligently to perpetuate an image of integrity, honesty and moral responsibility to the people of Spring Grove, but Darren believes his dad has created a schizophrenic personality to contend with a political life where out of necessity he must exemplify the virtues that are important to the voters. Darren knows too well he is a big hypocrite, a total phony, a regular Dr. Jekyll and Mr. Hyde. He demonstrates a righteously sincere personality for the citizens of Spring Grove and a controlling diabolic personality for his family.

How his mother manages to survive their household environment genuinely bewilders him. Maybe, it explains the cold wall she has built around herself, which keeps her oblivious to everything his dad says or does. She is always in her own little world with room only for Darren... for whom she lavishes her love and understanding. If it were not for his mother, he would have left Spring Grove years ago.

Darren slowly walked the long hallway to the mayor's office and with a strong push on the heavy door entered the outer office of the secretary, Mary Lee. She announced his arrival and he reluctantly entered a beautifully decorated office. He always marvels at the lavish furnishings, which create an atmosphere of opulence, and the thought goes through his mind: *For a servant of the people, my Dad sure enjoys the "good life"*. Darren was obliged to stand before the desk waiting to be invited to sit at his dad's request. It was just another way of his dad's commanding respect.

"Well, Darren, have a seat. I understand Mrs. Mason has asked you to investigate her husband's death. Why she would ask someone so inexperienced is beyond me." Mayor Doyle critically uttered.

"Maybe, Mrs. Mason has more confidence in my ability than in Spring Grove's stupid police department." Darren sarcastically retorted. He knew the meeting was already getting off to a bad start.

"Now, watch it boy! You're talking to the mayor."

"Oh, Dad, I forget which hat you're wearing at times… the one offering fatherly advice or the one demanding respect for the office of the mayor."

"You just don't get it do you, son!" With this said the mayor stood up, leaned far across the desk and looked Darren square in his eyes and emphatically said, "You show me respect at all times no matter what hat I wear!"

There was a long period of silence. Neither one looked at the other. Darren started to get up to leave when the mayor breached the silence with a firm but quiet tone in his voice and with clenched teeth demanded, "I don't want you to take this case! Martin was a good friend of mine and I want the police to handle it."

Darren was quick to respond, "Not on your life, Dad. This could be the biggest case in Spring Grove's history and it could possibly launch my career as a private investigator. I plan to give it my best shot. If I can solve this murder, perhaps the good citizens of Spring Grove will know I'm not a goof-off as you have so ably convinced them." With a curious look on his face, Darren continued, "Why is that, Dad? Why do you hate everyone in our family?"

Darren jumped up from his chair before his dad could say anything and slammed the office door behind him startling the secretary. The mayor grabbed for the doorknob and pushed the door open, hoping to catch Darren. His face was red with anger and the stern expression melted to a soft grimace when he noticed Mary Lee looking at him in bewilderment. He quietly murmured to himself, but loud enough for the secretary to hear, "Some children take longer to grow up."

Mayor Doyle was not happy with their aborted meeting. It was another in a long line of meetings that had turned to a confrontation and then had ended abruptly. He returned to his office to contemplate his next move. His heart was racing and he could feel his blood pressure rise. He placed his fingers on the pulse at his wrist and started counting, checking the rate of his heartbeat. He fell into his chair livid with rage.

Chapter Four

The azure blue sky was in great contrast to the bleak, somber atmosphere surrounding Mason Manor, where members of the immediate family gathered for the reading of the will. Decorations in the atrium from the dinner party a few nights before looked conspicuously inappropriate as a heavy veil of grief shrouded the entourage as each filed into Martin Mason's study.

Time passed slowly for the solemn group. It was extremely difficult for each one to maintain such a grievous emotion -- with some able to produce tearful eyes -- when, in fact, no one in the room felt any love for Martin Mason. Each one, at some time or another, had wished him dead.

Darren stood quietly in the far back corner of the smoked-filled study next to the bookcase, trying to be as inconspicuous as possible.

Each one was consumed with internal thoughts of hopefully inheriting a fortune of mass proportions. All appeared extremely nervous while some puffed on cigarettes as if drawing life and strength for the impending reading of the will. Darren did not believe anyone present was concerned with who killed Martin Mason, but rather who would get the lion's share of the estate. Each one slowly scanned the room trying to figure out what, if anything, each would inherit. When their eyes fell upon Darren, he thought: *If icy stares could kill, I'd be dead.* He released his nervous tension by fidgeting with the car keys in his pants' pocket, creating a catchy repetitive soft jingling sound. Everyone quickly turned to focus upon him with mean, curious eyes trying to determine what his purpose is for being at the reading of the will. He quickly gave a nod of apology for the disturbance, wishing he could vanish into the woodwork. He did not understand the reason for his being present. Mrs. Mason requested that he attend, which request totally baffled him. He was beginning to think everything about this case was baffling.

Mrs. Mason was the only one sitting on a chair in front of the desk with her back to everyone present. She wore the appropriate little black dress with her hair pulled back in a sleek bun. She sat quietly, fully aware all her actions were being observed while wiping the tears from her eyes.

Rather than sit, Martin Mason's three children stood close together at the back wall, leaning against the credenza for support while sipping coffee. So many thoughts were rushing through their minds. No one showed any signs of grieving, as each one reflected upon that last unforgettable short meeting when harsh words were spoken.

There is no loyalty or sibling love among the three children. The fun years of youth are gone, and now how much money each one will inherit is the important dividing issue at hand… and in the past week, all of them had angered their father.

Chapter Five

... two weeks earlier

They are no longer children, although Martin Mason persists in talking to them as if they are. All three are in their twenties... Martin Junior is older than the twins; Jennifer and Kathryn have just graduated college; and each one dreads the inevitable frequent lectures in the *temple of doom*, which is Martin's study.

"Okay, Kat, what did you do now to initiate this cozy chat?" Junior sarcastically asked.

"Why do you think I'm the only one who can cause trouble in our family? You're certainly no angel!" Kathryn barked back.

"Cool it!" Jen yelled. "Let's wait and see what dad has to say. It must be something pretty serious as he has been acting very strange, lately. But who knows, maybe it's his new young bride who has him in a dither. I bet she's going to be high maintenance."

The door to the study was forcibly opened and Martin stood for a few seconds glaring at his three children. With a look of determination on his face and a strong stride in his step, he marched to his desk to sit down. The scene was reminiscent of all previous meetings with his children; and with slow, deliberate speech, he began.

"How did you do it, Kathryn? My wife's diamond necklace is missing and I know you have sticky fingers."

"Dad, give me a break! Just because I took some money from your wallet a few times, that doesn't mean I am a habitual criminal!" With further irritation in her voice, Kathryn mockingly scolded, "And I suppose you're talking about Mom's diamond necklace that your young bride was wearing last week." Nothing was said for a few seconds while they continued to stare at one another; and she pleaded, "Come on, Dad, what are you doing? You know Mom's jewelry belongs to Jen and me... and not to your greedy bride. Why would I steal something that is rightfully mine?"

Martin stretched tall with shoulders back as if bracing for battle and strongly urged Kathryn to remember, "You had better soften your tone of voice when talking to me... and who I married is none of your business. What I do with your mother's jewelry is none of your business. M*y money is my money! And what... and if you will inherit anything is my business.* And don't think you've hidden your drug addiction from me, either... I've known about it for some time."

Kathryn was dumbfounded to learn her dad knew she was using meth. She thought she was concealing her habit. She sat quietly with a tragic look of surprise on her face, while the strength drained from her body... and she said nothing.

Martin admonished, "We'll talk about this later!"

Jen put her hand on Kathryn's arm to sooth her emotional frustration. "How could you do it, Dad? How could you marry such a young woman! She's only two years older than we are. That's too creepy! Who knows, maybe she is going to stash things away for herself and blame us for everything."

"Well, Jen, my new bride has brought happiness into my life, which I haven't known for a long, long time, and I'm not about to listen to any accusations from you or anyone else, which could destroy my marriage. Have I made myself clear?"

Martin stood up from his desk and pranced around the room running his fingers through his thinning hair while everyone sat quietly. His mind was racing with how he should present his next question to Jennifer. He decided to be straightforward with his request, "Jen, I know you have had short romances in high school and college, but I want you to give some serious thought to getting married."

"Oh, really, Dad! And why is that?" Jen gave a silly little nervous laugh and asked, "Are you an authority on marriage, now? And I guess you have someone in mind." Jen's nervous laugh changed to a serious chuckle.

"Yes, I do." Martin pressed on to implore, "I want you to marry Peter Fletcher. You know he has always adored you since you were a little girl and he has expressed his desire to make you his wife."

Jennifer jumped up from her chair and yelled, "Dad! You've got to be kidding! He's your friend and I grew up calling him Uncle Peter." She fell over the pillows on the sofa crying, "No! No! That will never happen!"

Martin looked at Jen with adoring eyes. She has always been his favorite and he does not want to alienate her, now. The request is too important. He kneels beside her at the sofa and places his hand on her shoulder while she continues to cry. As if sharing a secret and taking her into his confidence, he whispers, "Jen, listen. He's my old friend and the best lawyer anyone could have. He's proved himself invaluable in many sticky situations with the government. My financial empire has grown because of his ability to satisfy certain problems." Martin paused to reflect upon his present concern and continued, "I am worried about a business transaction that is on the table for discussion before the board of directors and I want to be certain that Peter will vote with me. A union in marriage would further solidify the growth of my companies and it would ensure a good long working relationship with him." Martin pleaded, "Jen, I'm only thinking what would be best for you and for your inheritance."

"Dad, why do you always have to play the inheritance card?" Jen cried. "But you're right, he is your old friend. He's more than twice my age." She cried louder, "Never, never! It's not going to happen."

With a sly, mean stare, which penetrated right through Jen, Martin asserted, "Power and riches come with a price... and don't you forget it!"

"Dad, I know you will step on anyone to get your own way, but I will never agree to marry *Uncle Peter.*"

Jen and Kathryn both stormed out of the room leaving only Junior still sitting in his chair.

***

Martin Junior learned at an early age his dad's money could buy him out of trouble when necessary and the police department has a thick file on his many misdemeanors. Junior believed college was a wasted four years, except he enjoyed living the free and easy lifestyle of partying and playing poker into the wee hours of the morning... and his dad paid all the bills. His antics in college, however, were of a far more serious nature and his clownish extravagance for gambling and losing large sums of money is well known by everyone in Spring Grove. His most recent run-in with the police department involved his being a suspect in cooking and selling the popular drug methamphetamine. Once again, Martin's good friend Mayor Doyle helped to exonerate Junior of all charges. It is Junior's devil-may-care attitude toward life and money that concerns Martin.

Martin approached his feckless son from across the room, speaking in a strong, authoritative voice, "I want you to work as a sales representative in my district office in Italy. You graduated college three years ago and you still don't have a steady job. It's time you had some direction in your life and took responsibility for your own actions. I'm tired of bailing you out of every bad deal and babysitting your financial needs, which keep spiraling to an unfathomable amount of money."

"Dad, I haven't tried to get a permanent job because I thought you were going to give me a position in the corporate office! I've been waiting all this time. You promised if I graduated with good grades and proved myself worthy to inherit the business, you would give me a position in the corporate office. Why did you make me study so hard in college to get a degree in business and finance if I'm to sit in some distant country to be a salesman?" To reinforce his statement he repeated, "And if you recall, I was on the dean's list for

18

good grades." With a nonchalant attitude, Junior continued, "Dad, do you ever speak some version of the truth."

"Well, son, I think my threat to you of being disinherited if you could not prove yourself worthy of making good grades was enough to encourage you to study. I gave you every chance and even continued to pay all your bills; and you did prove you are smart, but you're lazy and spoiled."

Junior sat for a few minutes staring into space with a glazed look playing over and over again the word, "disinherit". His mind rambled: heaven forbid… no money. That would be a fate worse than death.

Martin hated it when Junior stared into space with a blank look and demanded, "Look at me, Junior! I'm cutting off your monthly allowance." And in a slow, belabored speech he continued, "I'm tired of paying for your gambling habits."

Junior knew from past experience this was not the time to say anything, but to sit quietly and let his father vent his anger.

Martin straightened up to stand tall and emphatically said, "It's time you face up to your responsibilities and be a man. Quit coming to me in a pathetic weakness pleading for money. Beginning now, you make your own way. You have two weeks to get to Italy".

Martin stormed out of the room.

Junior was stunned by his dad's threats. He didn't see it coming. He sat for quite awhile growing more furious with each passing thought. Then his face brightened: *Well, at least I will be far away from dad while living in Italy… and there are some great gambling casinos in Europe.*

Chapter Six

Time passed slowly for Darren while he continued to stand quietly, leaning against the bookcase awaiting the reading of the will. He turned his attention to the two gentlemen in the room who have been huddled together on the sofa whispering the whole time. He has never met them personally, but knows them by reputation as being two of the most influential citizens in Spring Grove. The older man is Martin's brother Stephen, who contributed the seed money in the early years of building the corporation; and the younger man is Richard Mason, Stephen's son and Martin's nephew, who is the chief financial officer for the parent corporation.

Darren reminisced about his high school days when he shared a few classes with each of Martin's three children at one time or another. Jennifer and Kathryn are identical twins who enjoyed playing games in school by switching identities, which exasperated a few teachers. They are both quite tall, very attractive having the same physical features and voice inflections, but their dispositions and personalities are severely different. He recalled that Jen was the football queen and social butterfly in school and Kat was the sports jock. He remembered Junior for his athletic ability and his arrogant attitude. Other than a quick "hello" their paths never crossed.

He was amazed they stood quietly without so much as turning to speak to one another. He thought, maybe they were embroiled in their own deep grief for their dad. He could feel their tension intensifying as each passing moment brought them closer to the reading of the will. With the sound of voices from the hallway, everyone turned to look at the door as it slowly opened.

Finally, the attorney entered the room.

***

Peter Fletcher arrived an hour late, as was his custom to make a grand entrance for the reading of a will. His plenary power afforded the privilege of commanding such importance. Peter swaggered into the room like a boxing champion parading around the ring, deliberately making eye contact with everyone. He was extremely tall, commanding a presence as he flaunted his height to the point of intimidating anyone of shorter stature. He was about to indulge in the reading of the will, and he basked in the glory that he was an important player in attributing to the success of Martin Mason's huge financial conglomerate. He felt it was appropriate to read the will and to distribute the financial empire from the desk where most of Martin's business transactions had been conducted. It did not bother him that just a few days before Martin lay dead on the desk.

He could sense the nervous anticipation of all members present and he alone held the papers that would determine everyone's future. He delighted in their frustrating anxiety and graciously assumed the arrogance afforded by the situation. He took a position behind Martin's desk, standing in silence for some time not wishing to break his mental sojourn into the past while thriving on the drama and milking the scene for all it was worth. There were so many memories.

His law firm had served Martin Mason faithfully for many years -- more years than he cared to remember. Peter and Martin were a crafty duo who could negotiate any business concern into a financial victory. Between the two of them, they were able to anticipate action required to maintain a strong financially sound business position thereby blocking any significant problem that may arise. Together, having the same devious, unscrupulous minds, they created a financial empire.

With a whimsical smile, Peter fiddled with the lock on his briefcase for a few moments to delay the reading of the will longer and to irritate the eagerly awaiting recipients. He was a master of manipulation and he enjoyed the feeling of power whenever and wherever he could get it. The scene was set. He took one last long look around the room at the gathered hopefuls who were anxiously awaiting the plight of their future. He did a double take when he saw Darren standing in the back of the room and questioned, "What are you doing here?"

Darren looked to Mrs. Mason for the answer with an expression that was pleading for help.

Mrs. Mason quickly answered, "I insist he stay for the reading of the will!"

A multitude of perplexing thoughts rushed through Peter's mind. He was bewildered and briefly lost his bearings as to why Mrs. Mason would want the mayor's son to attend the reading of the will.

"I hired him to find out who killed my husband and I want him to hear the contents of the will." Mrs. Mason emphatically stated.

"Oh, yes… that's right. Darren is a private investigator, now." And with a nonchalant shrug of his shoulders, Peter slowly read the short paragraph of the will with as much drama as propriety would allow… and he loved every minute of it.

Chapter Seven

"That's it? That's all there is?" Kat yelled and burst into tears. "You mean I am going to get only a measly four hundred thousand dollars?"

"No, my dear. You weren't listening." Peter scolded. "The four hundred thousand dollars is to be divided among the three of you each year until you reach thirty years of age... at which time you will inherit a percentage of your dad's financial holdings, which will also be divided among the three of you."

"That means Junior will inherit his share before Jen and me... since he is three years older." Kat cried.

"Yes, that's right." Peter continued, "And then you and Jen will divide the four hundred thousand dollars between the two of you until you reach thirty. It's all very simple."

"You mean if Junior dies before he is thirty, Jen and I will divide the whole four hundred thousand dollars between the two of us... as well as the larger inheritance when we are thirty years old?" Kat questioned.

"That's right!" Peter acknowledged.

"Hey, wait a minute. Quit talking as if I were not here... or dead!" Junior demanded and quickly stepped to the front of the room to stand by Peter. "First let's get one thing straight. No one is to call me Junior anymore! I've had enough of that name, and I don't want you to call me Martin, either. I'm not a 'chip off the old block'. From now on, you call me Marty!" He glanced around the room making eye contact with everyone as if to reinforce his request.

Mrs. Mason, Stephen and Richard sat quietly while listening to Marty vent his anger. Each one sustained a staggering blow of betrayal, believing Martin would be more generous. Millions upon millions of dollars were at stake and Martin doled out only a pittance of his wealth. The bulk of his estate was to remain in the company for future growth.

Everyone was quiet and Marty continued, "Why all the long faces? You really didn't think our dear ol' dad would make it easy for us to get our hands on his money, did you? Who knows, maybe the twins will die and I will get the whole four hundred thousand dollars for myself; or better, at thirty, I would get the percentage of the financial holdings all to myself. I think the game he wants us to play is rather clever. It would be ironic, though, if we were all killed trying to outwit one another."

"What a sweetheart of a dad we had." Marty murmured sarcastically, "He deserved to be killed."

"Uncle Peter," Jennifer asked with emphasis on the 'uncle', "of course, we will continue to get our monthly allowance, also… right?"

"No, the allowance is to be discontinued immediately." And in a pundit manner Peter instructed, "Martin believed you should all learn how to make your own way in this world, as he did. He said, 'It builds character'."

"It builds character? Ha! His three children don't know the meaning of the word!" Mrs. Mason emphatically stated.

"Listen who's talking! You're a trophy wife with barracuda instincts," Kat retaliated, "and you can quit crying, now. We all know why you married our dad. For just four months of marriage you did pretty well. The chalet in Aspen is probably worth a few million dollars plus your weekly allotment."

"Oh, yeah, sure." She sarcastically assured, "and with no money to maintain it! I can't live on five thousand dollars a week… I'll have to sell."

"Yes, you could do that or you could sell our mother's jewelry... which seems to have disappeared!" Kat bellowed so everyone could hear.

Jennifer quickly added in a coy, soft voice, "You can always marry Peter Fletcher."

"All right... that's enough!" Peter shouted, while looking directly at Jennifer. "This meeting is over. I have read Martin's last will and testament and you all know what you will inherit. I am going to execute and dispatch all conditions of this will, immediately."

In a fit of anger, Peter hurriedly stuffed all the papers into his briefcase; looked at no one; took long strides across the room to the door and slammed it behind him.

Everyone was in a daze of disbelief and said nothing. Once again, Darren released his nervous tension by fidgeting with the car keys in his pants' pocket. In a state of frenzy, they all turned to Darren and together compulsively asked, "What are you doing here?" Everyone was emotionally agitated to the point of becoming violent.

Darren said nothing and hurriedly left the room before anyone could ask any more questions.Mrs. Mason quickly walked out behind him. She forcefully grabbed his hand and together they scrambled to seek a quiet place outside where they could talk without fear of being seen or overheard. When they were out of sight from the house standing in a large grove of cedar trees, Darren demanded, "Why did you ask me to be present for the reading of the will?"

"Oh, it was awful, wasn't it? Now, you know what I have had to endure with those spoiled brats these last four months." She became more frustrated with her inheritance with each passing second and continued, "Can you believe that!" She abruptly raved in a sharp, shrill voice, while stamping her feet on the ground, "Martin promised he would take good care of me in his will."

Darren quietly injected, "Well, inheriting the chalet doesn't seem too shabby."

"Oh, I guess he wanted to give the chalet to me because he proposed to me there. But that's nothing compared to his millions... or probably billions. There are only a few people in his financial empire who know the extent of his wealth… and I know Peter is one of them and I assume Richard knows since he is the chief financial officer of the whole conglomerate. There has to be more to the inheritance than what was stated in the will… and only Peter knows.

"I think the person who killed my husband is still sitting in the room, and we must not exclude Peter. One of them may not have pulled the trigger, but you can bet one or more was involved in planning it."

Darren noticed there were no tears for her husband as she was consumed with anger for what she considered her small token of inheritance. The two stood quietly while Darren waited for Mrs. Mason to breach the silence.

"I'll admit I thought marrying Martin would be my easy ticket to a life of splendor… and why not? I pledged to be a wife who would comply with all his sexual desires; provide companionship; attend to the functional, mundane responsibilities of running a household; and masquerade as his trophy wife at all social functions."

Darren felt she wanted to bare her soul and stood quietly while she continued. "He told me how much he loved me and he wanted me to become a part of his life. He said he was surrounded by unscrupulous, corrupt people in a money-mad world and that I made him happy… and he asked me to marry him." She nervously twisted a small section of her long hair with her fingers; looked slowly off into the distance and repeated, "He loved me." She started to cry, "He knew I did not love him, but he said that it made no difference. He asked only that I be loyal and faithful to him… and then he would give me the moon and the stars… and he promised he would be generous to me in his will." In a contemplative mood she turned to Darren with tears in her eyes and asked, "What was I to do? I know what poverty is and I vowed I'd never be poor, again. So, I agreed to marry him."

Darren listened attentively to the story, but he did not know how much of it he could believe. He remembered how she came on to him in the study the day of the murder. He questioned, "Why do you feel you cannot live on five thousand dollars a week? That's a whole lot of money to me."

"Martin wanted me to join all the socially important charity organizations as he felt it would bring him more prestige in Spring Grove. In four months time, I have already pledged over three hundred thousand dollars and that does not include membership in the Cedar Valley Country Club, and this was all done with Martin's approval."

They heard the rev of motors in the driveway as they watched the others leave the house. Mrs. Mason regained her composure, turned to Darren, and with a strong handshake thanked him for coming. With an urgent sound in her voice, she asked, "I want you to keep me informed of the investigation. I want you to tell me everything… no matter how insignificant you may think it is." She hesitated a moment and then continued, "The police department has concluded its interrogation with me, but asks that I keep them informed of my location, so I have decided to go to my newly acquired chalet in Aspen. I will call you when I get there and give you my phone number." With a slight smile and a twinkle in her eyes, she whimsically mentioned, "I may as well start enjoying myself."

Nothing was said for a few seconds as they both stood watching the last car leave the driveway. A soft breeze whistled through the cedar trees with the sunrays casting gray shadows onto the expansive green lawn.

Once again, Mrs. Mason pressed seductively closer to Darren and asked, "Please don't call me Mrs. Mason. My name is Eileen. With nary another word spoken, she slowly meandered up the hill to the house. Darren thought: *I don't know which of her two personalities I can trust: the one that exemplifies the bereaved widow or the one that is the cold and calculating trophy wife. This lady really baffles me.*

Chapter Eight

The twins have a rather small condo located on the outskirts of Spring Grove. Their dad bought it for them several months ago as a college graduation gift, which also afforded him the opportunity to live in Mason Manor alone with his new bride. The condo is nothing lavish or grandiose like Mason Manor, but it is comfortable with three bedrooms, two and one-half baths… and the twins own it. There are certain amenities, such as indoor and outdoor swimming pools, club house, tennis courts and an exercise room. Both needed their weekly allowance to afford the basic necessities and maintenance; and now after the reading of the will, it is imperative for them to develop a financial plan so they will be able to afford the rich lifestyle they have known all their lives. Extra money was always available to them upon request; but, of course, there were always certain demands placed upon them by their dad, which they always managed to negotiate. The last several months before their dad's murder were the most difficult times when he would explode in anger with his children, but he was always sweet and soft spoken to his new bride… everything changed after he married.

Jennifer and Kathryn returned to the condo after the reading of the will, kicked off their shoes and collapsed on the sofa. No words were spoken as they tried to understand what had just happened. The silence was interrupted when there was a knock at the door. It was Marty.

"Are you still in town? I thought you'd be home packing to go to Italy." Kat asked.

"Oh, that," he slovenly answered. "I guess I still have to go if I want to work in the corporate office someday." Marty looked around the room to find a comfortable chair to flop into; reflected upon the situation at hand and contemplatively posed his thoughts. "You know, dad had no business ethics. He believed all is fair in business with the end justifying the means... and he was up front about it. Everyone knew his position. With Uncle Peter and our 'dear' cousin Richard at the corporate helm to steer the company now, I think they're going to be a formidable, crafty duo to confront. I don't trust either one."

Jennifer and Kathryn shook their heads "yes" in agreement, but said nothing. It had been a long disappointing day, draining them of any emotional feelings, and neither one has the energy nor the inclination to comment when the hall clock chimed six. The same thought hit all three at once that they had not eaten anything since breakfast. Jennifer went into the kitchen to get a bottle of wine while Kathryn rummaged through the refrigerator and kitchen cabinets for some snacks.

Marty put on a selection of CDs on the Bose to help create a more cheerful atmosphere, but the three continued to sit quietly immersed in their own thoughts.

Jennifer filled her glass with the last drop of wine and volunteered, "I'll go downstairs and get another bottle from the closet."

Kat and Marty took the opportunity to be alone to move closer to one another to whisper, as Marty turned up the volume of the music. "Have you unloaded the necklace, yet?" Marty anxiously asked.

"I'm working on it." Kat quickly whispered and continued, "Did you get in touch with Jake?"

"Yeah, Jake's going to Italy with me to test the market for meth." Marty responded.

Marty and Kathryn quickly returned to their seat locations when they heard Jennifer calling from the stairs, "I wonder why dad was so insistent that I marry Uncle Peter. Something pretty serious must be happening in the company for dad to even suggest such a ridiculous idea." Jennifer entered the room to the music blaring on the Bose and jokingly sang a rap to the beat: "The music is rockin' and oh so loud, but your faces are covered with some dark cloud." She started to laugh, "Oh, my, what long, sad faces". She opened the bottle, started to pour the wine and in a more serious voice continued, "You know you don't have to put on an act for me. I know you both are glowing inwardly with happiness that there will be no more lectures in the *temple of doom*. We may have one thing in common… we're siblings, but partners in crime we're not. I didn't shoot our dear ol' dad, so that leaves the two of you as suspects." Jennifer always reveled in jokingly taunting her siblings, but this time not even the loud music could break the somber spell.

Marty viciously retorted, "Knock it off, Jen! I'll admit there was no love between us, but I didn't mastermind dad's murder." Marty reminisced for a moment trying to remember some happy event he shared with his dad and recalled, "I guess when dad gave me my two-wheeler for my birthday and taught me how to balance on my bike… yeah, that was the best time we ever shared. For me, it meant freedom to explore the neighborhood… and the feeling was great. I don't remember dad and me ever playing or doing anything together after that." In deeper thought, he quietly uttered, "That was just before mom died." He turned to the girls to express his thought. "Do you remember how unhappy he was… and for so long. He really threw all his energy into developing the business and that's when his whole personality changed."

Jen interrupted, "That's about the same time Uncle Peter started coming to the house. I'm not looking forward to seeing Uncle Peter ever again, but I know that will never happen. There is no way he can make me marry him. I don't care if the company goes under".

"Oh, sure, like you don't care if we lose our money!" Kat sarcastically yelled.

"Well, then, you marry Uncle Peter if money means that much to you. He has always had trouble telling us apart." Jen added in a hurtful manner, "Of course, with your raunchy complexion, now…." Jen stopped and looked closely at Kat's face and continued, "What's with the big ugly sore on your cheek, anyway. It looks awful!"

"Stop it, Jen!" Kat covered her face with her hands and began to cry.

"Both of you stop it!" Marty yelled over the loud music. "Don't you think we should be a little concerned with who did kill our dad? I'd put my money on the trophy wife. She may not have pulled the trigger, but I'll bet she planned it."

"No, she had more to gain by being married to dad." Jen volunteered.

In a whimsical droll Marty started to laugh, "With our qualified Spring Grove police department on the case, we may never find out. I've been in and out of the police station so many times I think it has a swinging door. It was never the policemen who even bothered to question me, it was always the mayor who intervened after dad had a little chat with him… and I am sure some money passed between them. I'll have to admit dad always rescued me. I guess I will miss him after all."

Kat wiped the tears from her eyes and reminded Marty that Darren had been hired by the trophy wife to work on the case. "Perhaps he will be able to find out who killed our dad. As I recall, Darren was smart in school; and if you remember, he was president of our senior class. From what I understand he is a pretty good detective."

"Well, anybody would be better than our stupid police department." Marty assured.

The three sat for quite awhile bantering about the efficiency of some of Spring Grove's policemen, who reminded them of Barney Fife, a character from an old TV show where he wasn't allowed to put a bullet in his gun. The three sat and laughed, and forgot about everything important. It was a nice respite from all their immediate problems.

It was late when Marty suggested, "I had better get going. I'm going to pack and make reservations to fly to Italy tomorrow. I'll call you with my flight schedule and where I will be staying."

Chapter Nine

It was late in the morning when Marty awoke to the sound of a knock at the door, which quickly turned into a pounding and an agitated voice calling, "Come on, man, open up!"

Marty stretched and twisted in bed for a few moments longer and then stumbled to the door. "Okay, okay. Hold on!" Marty knew it was Jake and he was in no hurry to have to discuss serious business at this time in the morning. The two looked at one another, nodded, but said nothing. Marty led Jake to the kitchen where he brewed some coffee and the two sat at the table to discuss their impending trip to Italy.

Jake is a new friend who Marty met at a Texas hold'em poker tournament in Las Vegas. They are the same age and the two have become quite close, sharing the same desire to make a fast buck the easy way. He is from a wealthy family in Oklahoma and he, like Marty, has grown up in an affluent environment. Together, they have decided to make their fortune selling meth to foreign countries.

Jake is involved with a large, scattered group of people in the Ozark Mountains in Missouri who cook the highly addictive stimulant meth, which is the poor man's cocaine. These mom-and-pop mountain dwellers do not stay in any one place too long, but move around the area to dodge the law. The cooking labs are called clandestine because meth can be made in small unobtrusive houses or buildings where no one knows the inhabitants are cooking meth with cheap, common household items and the rural areas provide great cover for the pungent chemical odor, which is released. Meth laboratories have grown to large proportions resulting in Missouri now being known as the meth capitol of the country and Interstate 44, which cuts through the center of the state, is the drug dealer's choice of highways to transport meth... and Spring Grove is located in the center of all this activity. With the growth and spread of this drug to foreign countries, it is proving to be a very lucrative business... and Marty and Jake want their share of the action.

"Our trip to Italy is at an opportune time to sell meth," Marty reported in a pundit style. "I recently read that Italy is a major transfer point for shipping drugs to other countries in Europe; and their director of operations of anti-drug police is greatly concerned with the rapid spread and use of cocaine. It is reported that sales are the greatest in the northern part of Italy where the wealthier industrial cities are located spreading all the way along the Po River from the Alps south to the Adriatic Sea. We will be at the right place at the right time to get crystal meth into the country." Marty rubbed his hands together in anticipation of selling a large volume of crystal meth. "We will fly into Milan, which is the ideal wealthy, industrial city where you can find a small apartment and make your pitch to the dealers."

Both men sat to discuss other matters of concern and both agreed they were going to make their visit to Italy a successful, financial venture. After a couple of hours, Jake excused himself to go shopping for a few items he needed for his trip to Italy and promised to return later in the evening so the two could go to dinner.

Marty sat at the table for quite some time sipping coffee and pondered his position in establishing a market for meth in Italy. He knows it is a dangerous business, which can necessitate his becoming involved with organized crime groups around the world. He did not know for certain how deeply involved he wanted to become... especially now that his father is no longer alive to bail him out of trouble.

He slowly rubbed his forehead as if trying to think more clearly when his thoughts turned to Kat and her smoking crystal meth. Her complexion is starting to show signs of her addiction and he knows it is imperative she seeks help immediately to kick the habit. He feels responsible for her addiction and regrets he offered her a smoke, which was laced with crystal meth as a joke… not thinking she would smoke it. He closes his eyes with the thought: *Kat has promised me she will check herself into a rehab center in Utah when she sells the diamond necklace. Hopefully, it will bring in enough money to pay for all her medical expenses without anyone learning of her addiction, as everyone here will think she is vacationing with some of her girlfriends.*

***

It was late afternoon by the time Marty was able to get in touch with his friend Carlo in Como, Italy. He wanted to coordinate flight schedules with him as to when Carlo could pick him and Jake up at the Malpensa International Airport in Milan. Carlo is a friend from high-school days when he was an exchange student at Spring Grove High School and lived at Mason Manor for his senior year. The two were "big men on campus" in football and track and a fraternal bond was woven of trust and loyalty. This friendship was easily conceived since both their dads were business acquaintances sharing the same large office building in Rome. Carlo is the third man in this newly established enterprise; and Marty is hoping with Carlo's knowledge of Italian and German languages, plus his birthright of living in Italy, certain obstacles will be easily avoided.

Releasing pent-up anxiety after his phone call to Carlo, Marty placed the phone receiver in its cradle with a smile on his face thinking: *Jake will concentrate on the availability of crystal meth from his friends in the Ozarks to the dealers; Carlo will plot out the locations throughout Italy for distribution centers and I will negotiate the sales and handle the finances. Oh, how sweet it is!*

***

It was early the next morning when the shrill ring of the phone startled Jen. She slowly turned in bed to answer with a low, breathy voice, "Hello."

37

"Jen, it's me. Jake and I are leaving for Italy this afternoon and I want to give you our flight schedule and where we will be staying for a few days before I go to Rome. Do you have a pencil and paper handy?"

"Wait a moment." Jen fumbled in the top drawer of the nightstand at the side of the bed for a pencil and a scrap of paper. "Okay, go ahead." Jen urged.

"We have a really lousy flight, as we have to change planes twice; once in Detroit and again in Amsterdam. Our plane leaves St. Louis this afternoon at 1:32 p.m. and we arrive in Milan tomorrow morning at 11:25 a.m. Carlo will meet us at the airport. He has made hotel reservations for us at the Hotel Villa Flori on Lake Como, which is only a short distance from Milan and the Swiss border. It is also very close to his parents' villa on the first branch of the lake."

Jen questioned, "Who is Jake? And why are you flying into Milan instead of Rome?"

Marty was startled with the question. He had forgotten he has never told Jen about his new friend Jake and their business venture… to sell meth in Europe. Only Kat knows.

"I met Jake a few months ago and we have become close friends. He told me he has never been to Europe and asked if he could travel with me to Italy and possibly hang around with Carlo and me for a few days before I have to report to the office in Rome." Marty felt this was a convincing story and continued, "I think you will like Jake. His dad owns oil wells in Oklahoma and he, pretty much, doesn't have to work, as he has already inherited a lot of money from his grandfather. Plus, he is really a good looking guy. Maybe, I should introduce you."

"No thanks!" Jen quickly and adamantly responded. "Please don't try to be a matchmaker like dad. I know I am going to have to face Uncle Peter pretty soon and I am not looking forward to the meeting."

Since Marty has been intensely preoccupied with planning his trip to Italy and his new business venture, all thoughts of his dad's murder and the problems with the restructuring of the corporation's board of directors have eluded him. The mention of Uncle Peter's name definitely sparked serious concerns for the future of the corporation. He also realized for the first time that with him in Italy and Kat in California, Jen will be the only one at home to follow the murder investigation.

In an uncharacteristic serious voice, Marty implored, "Jen, if anything comes up that you don't want to... or can't... handle by yourself, I want you to call me immediately."

Jen coyly laughed, "Gee, all this concern for your little sister... I'm shocked."

"I mean it!" Marty responded. "We don't know who killed our dad and we don't know why. There is a murderer running around out there who may want to kill us, too. As soon as I get to Rome, I'll call you with my phone number. Carlo and I are going to rent a small apartment close to the office. Take care."

Jen remembered Carlo from high school days when he lived at Mason Manor as an exchange student. She thought of how competitive they were and all the fun they had when playing computer games. As an after thought, she injected, "Tell Carlo 'hi'! Have fun and don't worry. I'll call Darren to find out if he has any leads in solving dad's murder."

Chapter Ten

Indian summer in the Ozark Mountains is a beautiful time of year to see the vibrant colors of deep red, orange and bright yellow leaves from oak, dog wood and walnut trees sparkle in the sunlight in the midst of groves of deep green cedar trees. The Cedar Valley River gracefully winds through the foothills and circles the estate of Mason Manor. Since the murder of Martin Mason, the house has been closed and the only residents are Wally, the caretaker, and his wife Della. Mrs. Mason has moved to her newly inherited chalet in Aspen; Marty is working in Rome and the twins have their own condo in Spring Grove. The mansion is owned and maintained by the corporation, and Stephen Mason, the deceased's older brother, is the executor of the estate. Jen's jetstream blue Corvette took the curves easily on the old country road leading to Mason Manor. Some curves are not banked properly, but she has driven the road hundreds of times and knows at what speed she can take each curve... and she likes to push it as fast as she can. With the top down and her long golden blonde hair blowing in the wind, she has a feeling of freedom that she loves.

Wally was at the front iron gate at the road to welcome her. Since the murder, it has been locked and the house has been closed to visitors. While she sat waiting for him to open the gate, she reminisced how she, Marty and Kat liked to play hide-and-seek with him. He, also, taught them how to ride horseback, rope a steer and herd cattle. She sadly thought: *I remember all the great stories he used to tell us about being a cowboy in Montana. Wally's old bowlegs don't move as quickly, now.*

"Hi, hon," Wally called, "why don't you drive on up to the house and I'll wait here for that detective fella to come."

With a big smile, Jen acknowledged, "Okay."

Della was at the front door to welcome Jen with a big hug and a kiss on the cheek. "I'm sure glad to see ya. Are ya feelin' fine?" Della asked, wiping her hands on her apron.

"Well, as fine as I can feel under the circumstances. I've asked Darren to meet me here. Hopefully, he has some leads to go on in his investigation of dad's murder."

Jen's eyes filled with tears as she started to cry. "Oh, Della, it's so awful. I still can't believe it. You remember how strict dad could get with us, and we hated him.

"You and Wally certainly know how mean he could be, and yet you continued to work for him. I often wondered why you stayed. I don't think dad had a real friend in the whole world." Jen lamented, "But you know what, Della, he was my dad and I do miss him."

Della put her arms around her in comfort, which reminded Jen of the times when she was a very little girl and would hurt herself. Della was always there with a Band Aid and an apron to wipe away her tears. Della had been her substitute mother for many years and it was her tenderness that made her cry. They stood for some time embracing one another and saying nothing when they heard the motor of Darren's car pull up at the front door.

"I'll go to the kitchen and get some iced tea for ya." Della offered.

Darren called as he stepped from the car, "Hi! Isn't this a beautiful day."

The two sat down on the front steps, marveling at the colors of the trees and looking around the manicured lawn of the estate not knowing how to breach the silence to talk about the investigation. Darren looked tenderly at Jen, "I want to offer my condolences. I didn't get a chance to talk to you at the reading of the will." His mood changed quickly and in total frustration, Darren raised his hands and exclaimed, "Hell! I didn't even know why I was supposed to be there! Mrs. Mason insisted that I come. Let it suffice to say it was an extremely awkward situation."

"Oh, yes, the trophy wife." Jen curled her lips in a smirk. "I'll never figure out why dad married her... and she's only two years older than I am. Oh, well, at least she's not going to live here. I understand she has moved to the chalet in Aspen." Jen surmised looking at Darren and posed the question, "How do you like working for her?"

"I'll let you know after I return from Aspen. She wants me to fly out there, as she says she has something important to tell me, but she doesn't want to talk about it over the phone. She thinks her phone is being tapped and..."

Della interrupted, "I'll put the iced tea on the porch table." She nodded to Darren and returned to the kitchen.

Darren did not want to divulge anything of importance to the case, but merely stated he was following several leads and he was most anxious to talk to Mrs. Mason. The two sat on the porch enjoying one another's company while the hours were slipping away quickly into evening.

The setting sun cast long shadows across the lawn when Jen realized nothing much had been discussed about the progress of the investigation. Most of the time was spent talking about high school days and mutual friends... and mostly they wondered why their paths had not crossed more in school. The dusk-to-dawn lights turned on illuminating the immediate lawn around the house. Darren realized he had an early morning flight to Aspen and suggested they meet to talk about the investigation after he returns from talking to Mrs. Mason.

Jen waved good-bye as Darren drove down the driveway; turned to walk into the house and was stopped at the screen door by Della. "He seems like such a nice young man. I don't remember seeing him before. He looks so young to be a detective."

"All I remember is he was the class president. At that time in my life, I had a big crush on Jack, but Kat really nixed that for me by going out with him... and he assumed he was dating me. Kat thought it was funny, but I thought it was a mean trick. She knew how much I liked him."

"Well, honey, why don't you come in and have supper with Wally and me? I have fixed a big pot of beef stew and we can talk more."

"Oh, Della, that sounds so good. I haven't had beef stew since I moved to my condo."

The three sat at the table playing catch-up with details of their present lives. "We figure it's about time for us to move on," Wally floundered in his speech not knowing how Jen would take the news. "We've worked here on your place since you were a baby… and, well… we've bought us some acres in Montana where we can breed a few horses." Jen was disappointed, but not too surprised they were going to move.

"When do you plan to go?"

"Oh, we'll probably hang 'round here for awhile, yet. At least until we find out somethin' about this investigation. Stephen Mason has asked that we stay to look after the place until things settle down; and he didn't say how long that will take." Wally got up from the kitchen table to look out the back door. The view down the hill was breathtaking as the moonlight danced on the Cedar Valley River painting a silver strand winding through the valley. "Well, it's for sure I'll miss this place."

He turned to ask Jen, "How are things going with you?"

"My interior design shop has been open about six months and I am really enjoying some good business. It was slow at first, but I think the wealthier residents of Spring Grove are getting used to the idea they don't have to go to a big city to find quality furniture and fabrics… and my partner Sally and I get along very well. So, I guess you could say I'm having fun." She looked at her wrist watch, "I didn't realize it was getting so late. I didn't intend to stay this long, but I really have enjoyed my visit." With a wave of her hand, Jen was out the door and hopped into her car.

The moon shone brightly on the black asphalt making it easier for her to drive on the dark, lonely road. She had driven only a few miles when she noticed a pick-up truck parked at the crossroads with its headlights glaring. She started to slow down to offer help if it were needed; but when she approached the crossroads, the truck jolted in front of her barely missing her car. She quickly swerved to the other side of the road and accelerated the gas pedal. Her heart was beating as fast as her car was racing. The truck immediately followed and together they drove at great-neck speed down the country road. It appeared the driver of the truck wanted to rear-end her car to force it into the ditch. Jen knew the dangerous stretch of road was coming up where there is one curve after another and she pushed the gas pedal down harder. Her little sports car performed beautifully at the curves, and she could see in her rearview mirror the truck was starting to weave. The truck could not take the road at the high speed. At the infamous "S Curve", the truck veered off the road into the field. About a mile farther down the road, where it straightens to approach the main highway, Jen noticed the truck was nowhere in sight. Nevertheless, she continued at great speed all the way to town. She pulled into her driveway, securely locked the garage door and frantically entered her condo. Her nerves were shattered, but she was happy to be home.

Chapter Eleven

It was after midnight when Jennifer placed a call to Darren. The sound of a phone ringing late at night is always magnified ten-fold... especially when the phone is on the nightstand next to the bed. Darren was enjoying one of his better dreams and he did not like being interrupted. He looked at the time on the clock and decided not to answer it; but his eyes glanced at the caller ID displaying Jennifer Mason, so he thought he had better take the call.

"Yeah, what's up?"

"Darren, it's taken me an hour to calm down so I could call you without babbling like an idiot. I was so frightened. I think someone was trying to kill me."

"What happened, Jen?"

"Someone in a pick-up truck tried to force me off Highway 8 after I left the house. I think he was waiting for me as the truck was parked at the crossroads."

"Did you see who was driving or can you describe the truck?"

"Well, I couldn't see who was driving, but the pick-up truck had the extended cab and it was a white Chevy."

"In this area, that narrows it down to at least fifty trucks like the one you describe."

Jen started to cry, "Why would anyone want to kill me?"

Darren asked, "Did you tell anyone that you were going to Mason Manor?"

"I mentioned it to Marty on the phone when he gave me his flight schedule to Italy. And, of course, I called Della to tell her when I was coming and that you were meeting me in the afternoon; and I asked her to let Wally know so he could open the gate."

"How about Kat? Did you tell her?"

"Kat flew out to Utah yesterday to visit some friends." Jen advised.

"I didn't want to tell you yesterday, but things are happening that I don't understand. The police department is dragging its feet in its investigation; and a few days ago, a water pipe broke in the department's evidence room destroying critical information regarding your dad's murder. My flight leaves at eight this morning and I will call you when I get there. I want you to be extremely careful."

Darren hung up the phone with a puzzled thought and recalled yesterday morning's phone conversation with his dad. It was another in a long line of bitter talks that ended abruptly. Once again, his dad vehemently told him to give up his investigation of Martin Mason's murder; and that he, as mayor, would see that justice would prevail. He ordered him to back off. In the course of the caustic conversation and in the heat of the moment, Darren told him he was aggressively pursuing his investigation and that he was meeting with Jennifer at Mason Manor that afternoon and was flying this morning to Colorado to meet with Mrs. Mason at her chalet in Aspen. He counted in his mind how many people knew Jennifer was going to Mason Manor: Marty, Della, Wally and his dad. He considered all of them as possible suspects who could alert the adversary to Jen's visit to Mason Manor.

There was no need to go back to bed; he knew he would not be able to sleep. Of the four, he knew very little about Della and Wally and decided to check into their background when he returned from Aspen.

He was greatly concerned this case was expanding... with the possibility to include others who may be murdered.

Chapter Twelve

It was the end to a smooth flight when the plane pulled onto the tarmac at Aspen-Pitkin County airport. Darren spent the time on the plane playing over the facts he knew about the case. His research on the internet divulged Martin Mason's extensive holdings are diversified to include pharmaceutical, electronics, real estate, construction materials, timber and oil. The corporation was founded by Martin Mason and his brother Stephen over twenty years ago and has grown to include offices and manufacturing plants throughout Europe. The parent company is called Double MM. Peter Fletcher, the firm's lawyer; and Richard Mason, the chief finance officer who is Stephen's son, joined the company eighteen years ago and are members of the board of directors. These four men, having plenary power and who are referred to as the Big Four in financial circles, created a financial empire, which is envied on Wall Street. Over the years, there have been government investigations into violations of the anti-trust law, fraudulent activities of rogue dealings in the stock market and money laundering, but these cases never went to trial... thanks to Peter Fletcher's clever manipulation of circumstantial evidence, plus lenient rulings and interpretations of laws by certain municipal judges.

The plane taxied to its gate at the terminal. With a carry-on, briefcase and map in hand, Darren was anxious to rent a car to drive to Mrs. Mason's chalet. He was confident he could find the chalet from the map Mrs. Mason had sent him. In her note she included a word of caution for him to be careful of deer on the road as this is the rutting season when male deer are more active. She explained there are many auto accidents each fall when deer become confused and jump into the path of a car. Darren kept this warning in mind as he slowly proceeded up the mountainside to the chalet, which is nestled on the western slope in the majestic Rocky Mountains. It was a circuitous route on a very narrow road demanding his full attention.

To his great surprise, there were many cars parked in the expanded driveway. TV cameramen were walking the immediate grounds around the house taking pictures while reporters and policemen were scrambling to hear details of the unseasonable intrusion of a grizzly bear in the chalet.

Darren did not know what to expect as he walked up the steep slope from the six-car garage to the chalet at the top of the mountain. His mind raced with different scenarios… and none of them were good. He pushed his way through the front door, knocking over a cameraman in his excitement to see inside. The circular Great Room, with an eighteen-foot beamed cathedral ceiling and a magnificent floor-to-ceiling faux stone fireplace, was totally trashed with a grizzly bear lying dead in the center of the floor. He quickly scanned the crowded room and was relieved to see Mrs. Mason sitting in a chair, but visibly shaking. He arrived in time to hear the neighbor tell the policemen what happened.

"My wife and I were sitting in the kitchen having breakfast when we saw this grizzly bear rollicking through our grove of aspen and evergreen trees as if it were on the scent of an animal. The bear appeared focused to stay on the pathway leading to Eileen's chalet. I have an extensive collection of rifles and grabbed my powerful Winchester Model 70, .338 Magnum and went after it. The bear was too busy forging ahead to notice me, although I kept at a safe distance with my rifle ready. I noticed there was garbage spread along the pathway that veered off to the dumpster at the back road. I think the bear and I saw the front door standing wide open at the same time. The bear took off running and I was right behind. There was a bloody hind quarter of a deer right inside the doorway. Of course, that was the scent the bear was following all along. Eileen was at the top of the stairs screaming hysterically while trying to dial her cell phone when the bear started to move toward her. Luckily, I got off two good shots and the bear fell immediately. Then I continued to pump more bullets into it… to make certain it was dead. Eileen came running down the stairs and fainted. I called 911 and then I called my wife to come up to help Eileen."

"Did the bear trash this room?" The police sergeant asked.

"No, I killed it before it could do anything." The neighbor replied.

"What did you say your name is?"

"I'm Roger Taylor and this is my wife Dorothy. We've lived here a long time; and when no one is staying at the Mason Chalet, we kind of look after things."

"So the room was already trashed when you came in?" The sergeant asked.

"That's right." Roger responded.

Darren stared at Mrs. Mason for a few moments as she sat cowering in a chair far away from the dead bear. The woman he believed to be a fortress of strength now appeared to be a weakened woman surrendering to shattered nerves.

The police sergeant walked slowly to Mrs. Mason; expressed his regret for having to ask her questions at this time, but proceeded. "Why don't you tell me what you heard?"

Mrs. Mason tried to gain control of her shaking body and began: "I was asleep upstairs when I heard a very loud growl and ran to the top of the stairs to see that bear ripping that deer to pieces." She said pointing to both animals.

"You did not hear anyone trashing this room or any other sounds prior to hearing the bear?" The sergeant pursued.

"No, I didn't. If you notice there are eight leaded glass windows in the two hallways leading from this Great Room. One hallway of glass leads to the master suite of rooms at the south of the main house and the other hallway leads to the bedrooms to the north. The suites of bedrooms are like satellite structures and are pretty far from the main section of the house. I think it was modeled from a Frank Lloyd Wright chalet, whose avant-garde designs are quite famous for integrating the interior rooms with the outdoors. No matter where you are in the house, there is a spectacular view of the mountains from nearly every window. When I am in the bedroom, it is quite difficult to hear anything from the Great Room. Plus, I did take a sleeping pill last night, as I have been having trouble sleeping lately."

"Do you have any surveillance cameras sweeping the grounds and do you have a security system?"

"Of course! Well… it hasn't been working for two days because the company couldn't get up here to fix it right away. I think it is supposed to be fixed tomorrow. You don't think someone purposely cut the electrical lines, do you?" Mrs. Mason pleaded… crying, "And why would anybody want a bear to come inside?" She became hysterical screaming, "Martin's dead! And now why does somebody want to kill me?"

With assurance in his tone of voice, the sergeant affirmed, "That's what we are going to find out."

The sergeant turned to Darren and asked, "What's your name and what are you doing here?"

Darren quickly produced his private investigator credentials and explained that Mrs. Mason had hired him to investigate the murder of her husband and…

Mrs. Mason interrupted, "Darren, I would like you to spend the night here with me as I will feel a lot safer to have you in the house. I've made reservations for you at a motel in Aspen, but I would really appreciate it if you would consider staying here tonight."

The sergeant shook his head in agreement, "I think that's a good idea."

***

It was late afternoon when the policemen and camera crews left the chalet. Roger and Dorothy volunteered to stay to rustle up some food for supper from the well-supplied kitchen. Mrs. Mason gave Darren a tour of the chalet so he could learn the layout of the rooms in case he should have to put up a defense against any intruder during the night. The scene was reminiscent of the two burglaries at Mason Manor. Once again, a room was trashed as if someone were looking for something.

Darren marveled at the opulence of the interior decorations. He is not surprised to see that Martin's good taste of expensive furnishings is evident in his mountain retreat. From the wrought iron and glass front door to the interior furnishings of each room resplendent with dark wood, jewel tones of hunter green, crimson, turquoise, gold and shades of brown, leather, stone and art creations … a theme of European elegance is created.

The spacious master suite of rooms of the one satellite structure was arranged to have two separate bedrooms with lounging areas and fireplaces linked by a beautiful master bath to provide Mr. and Mrs. Mason bedtime options, if one were a morning person and one nocturnal.

Mrs. Mason directed Darren to the well-stocked wine cellar with its custom-made arched wrought iron door with an iron trellis designed in a clustered grape motif. Darren was overwhelmed: *I can't even conceive of how much money it took to build and furnish this magnificent chalet.* He remained in a trance-like state absorbed by his thoughts when Mrs. Mason grabbed his arm. With two bottles of wine in hand, Mrs. Mason led him into the dinning room. Dorothy had supper ready on the table, while Roger had started to clean up the mess in the Great Room. The four sat down at the table to eat, but there was very little conversation. Each one was absorbed with thoughts of the day's excitement. Fortunately, the animal carcasses had been taken away, along with garbage from the dumpster.

Roger was the first to finish eating. He did not know how to breach the silence with a personal question. After staring for a few moments at an over-sized portrait of Martin Mason hanging above the antique carved oak mantel of the fireplace in the Great Room, his curiosity got the better of him and he asked, "Eileen, when I straightened the picture above the mantel, I noticed there is a rather large safe behind it. And, I wonder if you have thought to check to see if anything has been taken from it?"

"Oh, that safe. There is no need to look. There is nothing in it. Martin liked to call everyone's attention to that safe as he said it reminded him of old movies where all the valuables are placed in a safe behind a portrait above the fireplace. He would embellish upon the plot of the movies and then he would laugh. It was his little joke he shared with his friends. He, of course, made everyone believe it was true… that he kept his valuables there."

"That seems like a pretty sick joke to me. Didn't Martin realize that someone may take him seriously?" Roger inquired.

"Well, I guess you had to have known Martin. Sometimes, his little jokes were very cruel. He probably thought that someone would be pretty stupid to believe him."

Instantly, Eileen recalled several cruel jokes he played on his friends, but they thought Martin's jokes were bittersweet. He was the only one who ever laughed.

Had Martin been a poor man, Eileen knows for certain the person taking the brunt of his joke would have stopped him cold. It was because of his money he was allowed to make a fool of people.

Eileen went across the table to put her arms around Dorothy to thank her for offering support when she really needed someone. She turned to thank Roger when tears filled her eyes, "I don't know how to thank you. God knows you saved my life today. If you and Dorothy ever need anything, please come to me, first."

Darren sat quietly in the Great Room while Eileen said good-bye to the Taylors.

The horrifying events of the past two days were too much to fathom. First, Jen's narrow escape from being forced off the road and possibly killed; and now, Eileen's narrow escape from being killed by a grizzly bear. It was incomprehensible to believe both incidents were related.

Eileen entered the room and called to Darren to follow her. She led him to the master suite. "I want to show you something."

While they walked through the glass hallway, Darren thought: Which personality am I going to confront? *The bereaved widow or the trophy wife.* And in deeper thought: *Eileen is very attractive. Maybe I should relax and enjoy myself.*

Eileen stopped. "This is what I want to show you." There was a beautiful Karastan carpet designed in a patchwork of colors in the hallway at the entrance to the master bathroom. Eileen bent down and easily removed a two-foot square patch. Underneath was a rather large safe buried into the floor. She exclaimed, "This is the real safe." She removed some papers and handed them to Darren. "I want you to take a look at the contents in this safe. I think these papers are the ones someone has been trying to find."

"How long have you known about this safe?"

"After we were married, we flew to the Greek Isles for our honeymoon and then decided to spend another week here... where Martin proposed. This chalet will always be special to me." Eileen closed her eyes as if to relive the happiness she had come to know... with no more money concerns. In a soft, tender voice, she continued, "Martin wanted me to know where the real safe is located and he even changed the combination to my birth date so he would never forget my birthday." In a quiet murmur, "He really loved me." Within a moment's time, her emotions changed from soft and loving to harsh and critical. "Why didn't he leave me more money so I can maintain a style of living befitting owning this expensive chalet? It doesn't make any sense."

Darren stood quietly in the hallway thinking what a clever place to hide a safe. *Who would ever think to look under a carpet at the entrance to a bathroom?*

"As soon as possible after the reading of the will and after the Spring Grove police chief released me from being interrogated further, I flew up here to be by myself. I opened the safe immediately to see if there were any papers that required attention by Stephen Mason. I'm afraid when it comes to reading legal jargon, I become confused with all the rhetoric of the party of the first part and the party of the second part and so forth." She handed the contents from the safe to Darren requesting, "I would like you to study these papers tonight and you can tell me in the morning what, if anything, I should do. I definitely do not want to turn them over to Peter Fletcher. I don't trust him."

With an expression of fear and whispering quietly, she revealed, "I have never been as frightened as I was this morning. I believe the bear was to be suspected of trashing the Great Room; and I believe the bear was supposed to kill me... and for what reason? I have no idea." She remained quiet for a few moments while the expression of fear changed to one of tenderness.

Eileen moved closer to Darren, pressing her body firmly against him while he slowly wrapped his arms around her. When she tilted her head up to look into his eyes, she noticed for the first time how tall he is... and she kissed him. She quickly pulled away; gave the papers to him and immediately turned to go into her bedroom, closing the door without saying a word. Darren stood stunned in the hallway; looked down at the safe in the floor and wondered what had just happened... it was all over in a moment's time. He was sexually aroused and, yet, she left him standing there wanting more. *She's a handful.*

Chapter Thirteen

Darren awoke to a loud voice singing in the shower. At first he became disoriented, not remembering where he was sleeping. "Where am I? Oh, yeah. I'm in Aspen and that noise must be Eileen." With a shake of his head on the pillow and a smile on his face he thought: *She sure bounces back from tragedy fast.* It had been a long night for him as he studied the papers from the safe until three a.m. He was in no mood to have to get up at nine in the morning.

He started to cough, as was a morning ritual, while roaming the bedroom for his clothes. He needed a cigarette. He was startled when his bedroom door opened.

It was Eileen wrapped in a bath towel. "I thought I heard you. Come on and get up. I'm anxious to hear what you discovered from reading the papers from the safe. I'll rustle us up some breakfast."

Darren just looked at her bewildered... never knowing what to expect. He had to admit: *She looked pretty cute in that towel.*

They had finished breakfast and were starting to discuss the contents of the safe when there was a knock at the door.

Eileen opened the door, "Come in. I've been waiting for you."

She called to Darren, "Why don't you go with the electrician while he repairs the surveillance cameras and the security system. I'll wash these breakfast dishes."

The electrician was familiar with the electrical system in the chalet, as it was his company that installed the equipment some years ago.

Darren was still bristling with having to get up early and was in no mood to watch a repairman do his job. In an agitated voice he said, "Well, you sure took your good old time in getting up here."

"Hey, buddy, we specialize in handling our repair work within two hours of receiving the call. Do you think these rich people up here like it when all their electrical surveillance systems break down? They get plenty scared when that happens. It's just them against Mother Nature... and what or whoever prowls around. It's a lonesome feeling."

"When did you get the call?" Darren asked.

In a snide, disrespectful tone the electrician answered, "It came in at eight o'clock this morning."

Darren was surprised and shocked to learn that Eileen had lied about the time the electricity had shut down. He knew this scenario of events altered the whole investigation of this case... and the murder of Martin Mason. This new information opened up a new idea: perhaps the murder of Martin Mason; the incident of Jen nearly being forced off the country road and possibly killed; and now the narrow escape of Eileen being killed by a bear were not related, but were committed as individual acts for personal gain by more than one person.

"Okay, buddy, you're in good shape, now!" The electrician called.

Darren was jolted from deep concentration, "Great. I'll walk you to the door."

When Darren returned to the kitchen to talk to Eileen, he decided not to divulge everything he had learned from studying the papers. His comments were directed to the first papers outlining the formation of the company twenty years ago and then the revised papers when Peter Fletcher came on board as the firm's lawyer. He mentioned the deed to six hundred acres of valuable property at the outskirts of Spring Grove, which appeared to be in order... and he said nothing more.

He remembered very well his dad's involvement with the sale of that acreage as the *Spring Grove Herald* splashed the story on the first page accusing the buyers of using fraudulent means to acquire the property, thereby, forcing out the owners. It was his dad's testimony that cinched the case for the buyers, which necessitated an article be printed in the *Herald* recanting their position. It was after this publicity his dad was elected mayor of Spring Grove for his honesty in the case.

Darren became depressed when he saw a second deed to the property was revised shortly after the trial to include his dad's name as part owner of the six hundred acres. He did not want to believe that his dad gave false testimony in this highly publicized case. *I think dad is closer to this case than I want to believe.*

It was late morning when Darren left the chalet. Eileen watched from a window as he slowly drove down the road. She quickly turned to retrieve her cell phone from her morning coat and placed a call to Spring Grove.

The phone rang. A deep voice answered, "Hello."

In a stern, firm voice she began, "It wasn't part of our plan to leave the front door open so a bear could actually come into the house. Are you surprised I'm alive? The plan was to throw suspicion from me for the two break-ins at Mason Manor. I may have been a trophy wife, but I had nothing to do with those two break-ins. We agreed if I destroy Martin's copy of the property deed, you will stop throwing pernicious accusations my way, which distort the facts in the investigation of Martin's murder." Eileen cautioned, "Be careful! I may have to change our plan, again."

She slammed her cell phone closed while contriving a scheme in her mind. *You don't know I've already changed our plan. I have not destroyed the property deed. If you want to kill me, you are going to have to be smarter, because I'll get you first. Now, your son has seen your name as part owner on the property deed and he knows your testimony, which was crucial in swaying the jury's decision in the buyer's favor, was false. Who knows... maybe Darren will call you out and then I won't have to do anything.* She was happy with this thought.

Chapter Fourteen

Darren had much to mull over in his mind during the flight home. He knows his dad is not an honest person, which is pretty difficult for him to internalize since he is his father and he is the mayor of Spring Grove. Nevertheless, Darren now considers him a leading suspect in the attempted murder of Eileen Mason. He tries to put things into perspective: his dad knew he was flying to Aspen to talk to Mrs. Mason about new information regarding her husband's murder; after the turn of events at the chalet, he believes Mrs. Mason invited him so she could involve his dad with the murder of her husband concerning the valuable property they own together. He wondered if his dad and Mrs. Mason conspired to murder Martin Mason, as they both would have a lot to gain. His dad would be sole owner of six hundred valuable acres, which were recently zoned for commercial property, and Mrs. Mason would inherit a lot of money… and as it turned out, she also inherited a chalet in Aspen.

He carried the thought further: *if Mrs. Mason were killed, there would be no one else alive to testify that his dad's name had been added to the property deed after the trial was won in court by Martin Mason. Dad gave false testimony in that trial just as he is now making false accusations against Mrs. Mason. But where does Peter Fletcher fit into this scenario?*

When he opened the door to his apartment, his mind was whirling with questions to which he had no answers. He felt mentally drained.

The plane served no food and his stomach told him it was dinner time. A weekly ritual had been established when he moved out of the house, he would have Thursday dinner at home. His mother enjoyed cooking his favorite meals of stuffed peppers, pot roasts with oven-browned potatoes or one of many other tasty dishes, which afforded Darren with at least one good balanced dinner per week, and Darren looked forward to these weekly visits with his mother. She has told him many times Thursday night dinner is her highlight of the week.

He did not want to disappoint his mother, but there was no way he wanted to sit down at the dinner table with his dad, tonight. Not now! He envisioned his dad would ask many questions about his visit with Mrs. Mason pertaining to her husband's murder. And, maybe he would inadvertently divulge something during the conversation or maybe he would express something as inconsequential as a facial expression, which would alert his dad to Mrs. Mason's real intent for his visit.

Darren picked up the phone to call his mom to cancel dinner with a perplexing thought... what's a good excuse? when the doorbell rang. Darren was flabbergasted to see his dad standing at the door. The expression on his face prompted his dad to question, "You look like you have seen a ghost?"

"Oh, it's such a coincidence. I was just going to call mom to tell her I cannot come to dinner tonight." Hoping his dad would not stay long, Darren closed the door and stood in the vestibule to talk.

"Well, that's why I dropped by to head you off from coming home for dinner. Your mother and I are going to the city council employees' recognition dinner tonight. I have to preside over it... you know, award gifts for years of service."

Darren did not say anything and his dad continued, "I'm anxious to hear what new information you learned about Martin's murder." With a compassionate tone in his voice, he lamented, "Martin and I go back many years; we were very good friends."

This was a new sympathetic approach of questioning by his dad and Darren felt very uncomfortable. He started to fidget with the car keys in his pants' pocket and revealed only the story about a bear breaking into the chalet. He stretched the story to cover every detail as was told by the neighbor so his dad would think he was giving a full report.

"Was there anything of importance said regarding the murder?" His dad asked.

"Not really. Mrs. Mason found some papers in the safe pertaining to the founding of the corporation, but the papers really had no bearing on the murder." Darren answered. "She is paying me quite a lot of money to work for her and I think she wants to be certain I am still on top of the investigation."

"Well, that is really not much to report after flying all the way to Aspen for what I assumed would be important information." He looked at Darren for a few moments as if studying his face and with a sardonic grin added, "You know, son, you never have been a very good liar."

Darren became furious and yelled, "The hell you say."

His dad calmly reported, "The only time you fidget with your car keys is if you are nervous or if you are lying."

Both men stood glaring at one another with nothing being said. His dad forcibly opened the door and left Darren's apartment.

Darren was unnerved by the brief confrontation with his dad, which served only to bring a clash of dialogue in a face-to-face situation and deepened the chasm between father and son. A feeling of moral obligation swept over him, urging he should love his father, but he cannot justify pursuing an amicable relationship when his dad shows only a quarrelsome disposition. After this brief encounter, he believes his dad is deeply involved in this whole investigation and the thought of becoming a loving son sickens him.

Chapter Fifteen

Jennifer turned the key in the lock and stepped inside to a dark apartment. She stood there for a few moments realizing how very much alone she is. Her dad was murdered, Kat is visiting friends in Utah and Marty is in Italy. The silence was deafening.

She grew up in Mason Manor where dinner parties and charity events were the norm. Marty's crowd of young athletes along with the twin's girl friends always filled the house with fun and laughter. During the quiet times, when they were little, Wally would take the three horseback riding or fishing on one of the two big lakes on the property. There was always a lot of activity at Mason Manor, but things are different, now.

There is one redeeming factor in her new lifestyle, which makes her happy: she really enjoys her new business. Jennifer majored in art and interior design in college and her dad promised that if she made the dean's list, which she did, he would set her up in her own business. He bought a building in the new strip mall outside of Spring Grove and it was up to Jennifer to design the interior of the shop to accommodate displaying furniture, draperies, carpeting, fabrics, lamps and much more to entice the shoppers. She and her friend Sally run the business and the two had a great time shopping at the Merchandise Mart Building in Chicago and Dallas for everything necessary to complete a well-supplied interior design studio. She is determined to make her new business a success.

By habit, Jennifer quickly turns on all the lamps in the living room and puts on a stack of CDs of her favorite music... both help to create a cheerful atmosphere. She removes the hairpins from the french roll, which she feels makes her look more professional as an interior designer, to let her long blonde hair fall down her back. She kicks off her shoes and settles in a comfortable chair to relax for awhile before dinner.

With her eyes closed, many perplexing problems spin in her head when the phone rings. "Hello."

"Jen, it's Darren. How are you?"

"Right now, I'm sitting here with a myriad of stressful thoughts in my mind while trying to relax, but I'm glad you called." She quickly added, "I'm anxious to hear how things went in Aspen."

"I just got back in town this afternoon and if you haven't eaten, yet, what do you say we go out to dinner? I'm starving!"

"That's a great idea." Jen responded.

"I'll pick you up in a half hour." Darren's depressed mood after talking with his dad was greatly improved after hearing Jen's voice on the phone. His many troubling concerns with the investigation are always interrupted by thoughts of the afternoon they spent together at Mason Manor. She has even invaded a few of his dreams, which pleases him, and he looked forward to seeing her again.

"I'll be ready." Jennifer jumped up from the chair with the happy thought that she was going to see Darren. She changed clothes... from a business suit to a feminine dress, styled her hair and put on fresh makeup. She glanced at her reflection in the mirror with an approving thought: *Those few pounds I lost really do make a difference. I wonder if Darren will notice.*

***

Joe's River's Bend Steakhouse is located on a picturesque area of the Cedar Valley River. It was an exceptionally warm fall evening and the two chose to sit on the veranda where they could enjoy the ambiance of swinging lanterns from the cedar roof, which created a soft light on tables decorated with flowers and candles. It was a romantic setting.

It was difficult for Darren to concentrate on the investigation and his trip to Aspen, while sitting across the table from Jen. He rested his elbow on the table and placed his cheek on his hand staring at Jen the whole time and asked, "Were you this beautiful in high school?"

Jen blushed and with a little laugh posed, "That's a great line, but it's not very original."

"Ya can't blame a guy for trying." The two laughed and Darren continued, "I wanted to date you, but the word among the guys was you liked 'Jack what's his name', so we all shied away."

"Oh, yes... Jack" Jen scoffed with a flippant expression. "He dated Kat thinking it was me; and, of course, Kat led him on in his delusion, which she thought was funny. She knew I had a crush on him, but Kat can be mean sometimes." With a deep sigh of regret, uttered, "I can't believe I didn't say something to Kat at the time. That was the naive period of my life." With firm conviction, she added, "I hope I'm smarter, now."

The two were interrupted by a friendly "hello" from Joe... the owner of the steakhouse. "How's it goin'?" With a big smile, Joe extended his hand to Darren and winked at Jen, saying, "I'm not sure... which twin are you... Kat or Jen?"

"I'm Jen."

"I never could tell you two apart. It's great to see you both. It's been awhile since high school days."

Joe turned to Jen and offered his condolences for her dad's death and mentioned, "Your dad and his new wife used to come here quite often for dinner. They always sat at the table in the corner... I think they wanted to be alone. It was easy to see that your dad loved his wife"

Jen winced when she heard this as she had decided a long time ago she would never like anyone to be her stepmother.

"Well, I have to get back to the kitchen and I'll let you two enjoy your dinner. Try the prime rib, tonight. It's delicious."

The soft evening breeze blowing through the trees on the hills rustled the leaves to a lilting rhythmic sound with the katydids adding their shrill melody to the splash of the river's rapids spilling over the rocks from the hollow below. Jen and Darren enjoyed their dinner with nothing of a serious nature being discussed. The evening was too beautiful to destroy the peaceful, romantic setting with stressful conversation. They both needed a relief from their problems and they delighted in the feeling of freedom from worry if only for a brief interlude. They laughed at everything, which greatly helped them to relieve their tension. But with this façade of happiness, they both realized eventually they would have to talk about Jen's narrow escape from being run off the road.

Jen savored the last bite of cheese cake with coffee when she could not hold back the question any longer. "Do you have any idea who could have wanted to run me off the road? I've been playing that terrifying scene over and over again in my mind, and I have no idea who or why someone would want to do that."

"What do you know about Wally and Della?" Darren asked.

"They came to work at Mason Manor shortly after my mother died. Dad was devastated with grief and was advised by the doctor to take a few weeks off from work and he decided to vacation at one of those working ranches in Montana. That's where he met Wally and Della. He asked if they would want to come to work at Mason Manor where Wally would have complete control of the farm stock and would manage the whole operation and Della would take care of the house and cook. Dad offered them a big salary... in fact Wally always said they were over paid for doing what they loved to do. They love Mason Manor and care for it like it's their own. They have been like grandparents to us. Marty, Kat and I.... we all love them. I'm going to hate to see them leave." Jen was sad to say.

"What? When are they leaving?" Darren questioned.

"They bought some property in Montana where they will breed a few horses, but Wally said Uncle Stephen wants them to stay until after the investigation is completed."

"I understand Stephen Mason, your dad's brother, is the executor of the property, now. So, I guess Wally has to report everything to him. Is that right?"

"Well, Wally has always had a free hand in managing the property. My dad trusted him as an employee and as a friend." Jen suggested in a serious tone of voice, "Uncle Stephen wants to know everything that goes on here at Mason Manor. He even wants to know who comes to visit, and why, and when they leave. And Wally said Uncle Stephen gets adamant if Wally doesn't report everything... no matter how insignificant."

Darren pondered the thought, "Then your Uncle Stephen knew you were going to Mason Manor that afternoon to talk to me... and Wally probably reported to him when you left."

Both sat at the table quietly mulling over their thoughts for awhile. They were absorbed with the many possibilities of actions, which could be conceived with this knowledge.

Jen was startled with the idea and started to cry, "Darren, you don't think Uncle Stephen had something to do with wanting me run off the road... or even killed?"

"We don't want to jump to conclusions, but we definitely need to consider everyone as a possible suspect." In a nervous reaction, Darren fidgeted with his car keys and pleaded, "Jen, I want you to be extremely careful in everything you do or say. I'm beginning to think there are many people involved in this whole mess: your dad's murder, the attempt on Mrs. Mason's life, and the life-threatening incident you experienced on the road. The case keeps expanding."

Darren ordered another glass of wine for each of them and once again they sat quietly at the table engrossed in their own troublesome thoughts, struggling for a solution to Jen's grievous situation, which is the supreme concern. Darren's passionate desire to protect Jen ran rampant with the beat of his heart and he wanted to reach across the table, take her in his arms, and protect her from all harm. He had never experienced this strong desire for any woman... and he liked the feeling.

It was midnight when they left the restaurant to drive to Jen's apartment, which was a short distance, but Darren took the long way as he was in no hurry to say goodnight. Both felt drained from worry of the investigation, but both fully enjoyed the comfortable feeling of being together. As they strolled to Jen's apartment door, they gazed at the full harvest moon, which rolled across the sky evoking a sensual desire for young lovers… and Darren wished they were lovers. Jen turned the key in the lock, hesitating to face Darren to say goodnight, as she did not want the evening to end. In a slow deliberate move, Darren put his arm around Jen's waist and pulled her close. With eyes closed, they kissed passionately. Both felt the same heated desire to linger longer and they kissed again. They pulled back and tenderly looked at one another with eyes that betrayed a yearning for more. Darren gently cupped Jen's pretty face in his hands, tenderly kissed her soft, full lips one more time while they both reveled in the glorious moment. Darren whispered, "I'll call you tomorrow."

"I'd like that."

Jen lingered for a few moments with her back against the closed door. She did not want to break the romantic spell that rippled through her body. Her body and soul were relaxed with a feeling of complete happiness… a feeling she had never before experienced.

***

Darren left the apartment looking up at the bright moon with a small cloud passing over **and thought**: *So this is what love feels like!*

He paid no attention to a white Chevy pick-up truck parked a block away.

Chapter Sixteen

Italy

Carlo thoroughly enjoyed his senior year at Spring Grove High School as an exchange student from Italy. His father and Mr. Mason were business acquaintances sharing the same large office building in Rome, and Carlo was invited to stay at Mason Manor while studying in the States. Carlo and Marty quickly became friends having the same likes and dislikes of things, which are important to high school seniors; and college years continued to fortify the friendship. With the establishment of their new business venture of selling crystal meth in Italy, the two have grown closer, spawning a feeling of loyalty and brotherly love, which has no boundaries.

Carlo and Marty have rented a small apartment in Rome within walking distance to the Double MM district office where Marty will be a sales representative for the chemical division of one of the subsidiaries. This will establish Marty's entry position into the corporate office, which he hopes will lead to a seat on the board of directors as his dad promised. Working as a sales representative will provide excellent cover for his participation in developing the newly formed company for selling meth. Marty's responsibility will be to distribute meth shipments received from the States, which will be smuggled inside barrels of chemicals, which are regularly received by the subsidiary company. He also will handle the finances and will create a double bookkeeping system... one set to satisfy local authorities and one set for the sale and distribution of meth.

With the help of Carlo's father, Jake, the third partner, was fortunate to rent a   small condo, which is enclosed by the deep sloped Swiss Alps overlooking the blue waters of Lake Como. The only access to the condo is by boat, which is moored by a waterside entrance, and there is a cable car to carry residents up and down the mountain slope. He believes the condo is ideally located for safety purposes, if the need should arise from necessity to seek asylum from the Mafia or any criminal gangs selling cocaine. He will concentrate his efforts for selling crystal meth in the wealthy city of Milan, which is known for its fashion industry. Como is a short distance east from Milan and with Carlo's help, he also has learned his way around the wealthy industrial section of northeast Italy from Verona to Venice. Once he has exploited these areas for sales, he will expand his territory from the Po, Italy's longest river, down from the Alps to the Adriatic Sea in the south of Italy.

Marty, Carlo and Jake have the same temperament and easy-going disposition with regard to money. All three come from wealthy families, where large sums of monies are always available, and they are approaching their new business scheme with youth and inexperience in a vigorous manner to make a fast buck. The young male adrenaline is pumping in their veins and the three are eager to get started. Instead of calling themselves *the three musketeers,* as the three read The Three Musketeers by Alexander Dumas in an English literature class, they jokingly like to refer to themselves as the "three metheteers." To them, it will be fun and games... so they believe.

***

"I don't know about you two, but I think we need a break from work." Jake suggested.

Carlo started laughing, "What do you mean? We haven't started, yet!"

"Of course, we have. We have established our fields of operations: you and Marty have this tiny apartment in Rome and I have a beautiful condo on Lake Como." With a mystified thought Jake said, "Why did you rent such a small apartment?"

"You have no idea how difficult it is to find anything to rent in Italy… and most everything is small in size. We, Italians, know how to make every inch of living area work to its advantage. Space of private homes and commercial property is at a premium. Marty and I were lucky to find this apartment." Carlo felt like a professor teaching Jake about Italian-style living and offered, "Most vineyards are privately owned by families and are developed on small tracts of land. Like I said, we're scrunched for space."

"I guess I'm lucky to have a two-bedroom condo on Lake Como, which is surrounded by big Italian villas." Jake added.

"You can thank my dad for that. He owns several condos and villas in that area." Carlo reported.

Jake continued with his original thought, "Why don't the three of us take this weekend and go to Monaco where we can test our luck at the casinos?"

Jake marveled with the thought that Monaco is not considered a country, but is a principality, which operates the Place du Casino in Monte Carlo where the social life revolves around the gambling industry. "Can you imagine how much money is spent every day by foreign tourists who are anxious to unload their savings at the gaming tables? It must be a staggering amount!"

With a brilliant thought he suggests, "I think with all that money, Monaco should be called a kingdom instead of a principality."

The three chuckled at the stupid thought.

Marty reported, "Well, I have a lot of things I want to do before I start working at Double MM Monday morning. Why don't we just get a few of Carlo's friends and have a game of Texas hold'em poker Saturday night here at the apartment? We can order pizza, some snacks, and a few bottles of Chianti wine and celebrate the inauguration of our new business venture."

"Yeah, I have a couple of friends who know how to play the game," Carlo volunteered. "I think if there are five of us in this small apartment, it will be a crowd. My one friend is a real donkey when it comes to poker." They all laughed.

"He's still learning Texas hold'em and I don't know if he will ever understand the game. But once in awhile, he will win through dumb luck." Carlo continued, "He has a lot of money and he doesn't mind losing some of it." Carlo laughed, "And I don't mind winning it from him... it makes for a nice arrangement."

Jake asked Marty, "What do you want to do this weekend that is so important?"

"I thought I would check into buying a car. I can't believe these narrow streets in Italy... and you may as well forget parking. I'm glad I can walk to the office, but I still would like to have something to drive around Italy. I understand automobile insurance here is astronomically high because of all the auto accidents so I don't think I want a big car."

Carlo quickly spoke, "Why don't you buy a little Smart Car. I think just about everyone in Italy must own one. It's only about eight feet long by five feet wide by five feet high and you can pull straight into the curb to park. It only seats two people... so the three of us won't fit inside, but the insurance is cheaper and the car in American dollars only costs about fifteen thousand."

Marty added, "Yeah, I could buy a Smart Car or I could buy a Vespa motor scooter." Good naturedly he injected, "You have to learn how to cross a busy street all over again when walking in Italy... because if a Smart Car won't get you, a Vespa will."

The three laughed in agreement.

The three young men continued their good natured bantering for an hour, which helped to mask an underlying current of stress they are experiencing, but refuse to acknowledge. The challenge will be to operate a new drug business in Sicilian Mafia territory, but their stress is alleviated by confidence they can break into the drug industry by offering a cheaper alternative to cocaine, hoping to find a young market for meth.

They have spent long hours going over every detail and each one is cognizant of his responsibilities. Already, Carlo has proved to be a valuable asset in this enterprise. Through his contacts, he and Jake have hired a few men to assist them, but Marty will work independently, handling the finances. The old adage goes, "... all streets lead to Rome" and Carlo appears to know the important streets in Rome and in most of all the large cities. Knowledge of escape routes through busy streets is necessary and Carlo and Marty have spent long hours preparing for an urgent defensive getaway... if any danger arises.

The Spanish Steps, which is a tourist attraction and favorite meeting place in Rome, is within walking distance from Marty's apartment. More than one hundred thirty steps join Piazza di Spagna with the Church of Trinita dei Monti, which affords an ideal location for crowds of people to sit on the exceptionally wide stairs in the warm afternoons. The beautiful Barcaccia fountain is in the center of the Piazza at the base of the steps with many streets spider webbing in all directions from the fountain. The three young men decided this will be the safest and most convenient tourist attraction where they can discuss business with street-level associates.

The three metheteers are anxious to swing into action to get the business up and running, which will be the same day that Marty starts working for Double MM. With wine glasses in hand, the three make a toast for a successful hell of a ride and in a victory yell... pledge, "one for all and all for one."

***

Marty glanced at his watch. He figured it was a good time in the morning in the States to place a phone call to Jen, who should be working in her new design studio. "Jen! It's Marty. I figure it's about ten o'clock in the morning there... am I right?" Marty asked.

"Hi! Yes, I just opened the studio." Jen excitedly answered. "I've been waiting to hear from you. I want you to give me your address in Rome and the country phone code so we can keep in touch, but I'll probably e-mail you more often than call."

Marty was quick to respond to her questions and asked, "How is everything going at home? Have the police solved the murder, yet?"

It was a very long phone conversation as Jen was precise in every detail of her dad's murder investigation; of the attempt to kill their dad's wife, Eileen; and of her narrow escape from being run off the road by a pick-up truck. She mentioned the slow progress by the police department, and she spoke at great length about Darren and his ability as a detective; but to her dismay, nothing of importance had been uncovered.

Marty was greatly disturbed to learn about Jen's near-tragic incident on the road. His mind raced with possibilities of why anyone would want to harm Jen. His first thought was perhaps Kat wants Jen's inheritance. He quickly dismissed the thought as he could not conceive that Kat would want to kill her twin sister even though she will need a lot of money for the rehab center in Utah with its luxurious amenities and private rooms to help her kick her drug addiction.

In all sincerity, he spoke, "Jen, please be careful... and if you want me to come home to be with you until these mysteries are all solved, I will. We've had our share of disagreements, but I want you to know I will be there for you if you need me."

"Thanks, Marty, I appreciate that. Right now, I feel like I am all alone with no one to give me strength," Jen sweetly responded. "Usually, Kat and I can discuss things, but she is in Utah... and now you are in Italy." Jen started to cry, "Let's keep in touch... often."

The two said their good-byes. Marty gave second thoughts to his staying in Italy while both his sisters are experiencing psychological and emotional trauma. For the first time, he realizes with the murder of his father, he is now the head of the family. Responsibilities loom in his mind: he should take care of his sisters, at least until they marry; become the executor of Mason Manor instead of his Uncle Stephen; and assume his rightful position as heir to run Double MM. He feels there is a metamorphosis of his personality taking form initiating a genuine character trait of sensible, levelheaded thinking. He has never experienced this sober feeling. His dad used to remind him quite often he is smart, but he also scolded him for being lazy and spoiled. Marty rubs his head with his hand, hoping to think rationally... *perhaps, this is not a good time to be away from Spring Grove.*

Chapter Seventeen

Jen sat quietly crying in the back office of her interior design studio wishing Marty were back home so she would not feel so alone. She is in a state of depression, feeling like she has been abandoned: her dad was murdered; her twin is vacationing in Utah; and Marty is in Italy; and she is all by herself to handle any problems regarding the murder investigation. Her thoughts dwell on the scary incident on the road the other evening, and she cannot shake the lingering fear. She has had two deadbolts put on both the front and back doors and a security system installed, which help her feel a little safer, but she does not like living alone.

The tinkle of the bell on the studio front door alerts her that someone has entered and she quickly wipes her eyes, glances in a mirror to check her makeup and leaves her office. She is shocked to see Peter Fletcher standing inside by the front door.

"Good morning, Jen." Peter said cheerfully. He slowly glances around the room admiring the furnishings of the showroom, which exemplifies exquisite taste in color and design. "I can see you inherited your dad's appreciation of fine things."

"Good morning, Uncle Peter. This is a surprise."

The two were interrupted by Sally who was reporting for work. After introductions were made Peter said, "I thought maybe we could talk a little bit this morning, before you get busy with customers. I want to clear up a few doubts you may have about me. Can we sit in your office?"

Jen did not know what to expect, but braced herself for anything he may want to discuss. She just wished her frame of mind were better so she could think more clearly.

"I can smell coffee brewing. May I have a cup?" Peter asked.

"Certainly. I hope you like decaf." Jen was visibly shaking when she poured a cup and handed it to Uncle Peter.

"Are you okay?" He asked

"Oh, I'm fine." She nonchalantly answered. "Sometimes I start worrying about this horrible mess, and I keep thinking I'm going to wake up from a terrible dream."

The two settled down in comfortable chairs to talk, but nothing was said for a few moments. Jen did not want to start the conversation for fear that in her current mental state, she would become too angry to discuss marriage and she did not want to alienate Uncle Peter right away. She was anxious to hear what he had to say, first.

Peter looked at Jen with adoring eyes. He placed his coffee cup on the desk and began his story.

"Jen, I think there was a misunderstanding between your dad and me with regard to my wanting to marry you. You know I have been very fond of you since you were a little girl... as I have been fond of Kat and Marty, but the love expressed is as if you were my own children... in other words, it is a kind of love that a father would have for his children."

Peter stood up from the chair and walked to the window to look at the beautiful morning sunlight with eyes that were reliving past memories of bygone days, which imbued him to speak in a low, deep voice. "Jen, I have loved only one woman in my life with an unfathomable passion not even I understand. We had a love, which will span from now through eternity... and we pledged our love often. The night she and the baby died destroyed my desire to live." Peter choked back tears and whispered, "I guess it was your dad who saved my life, and our friendship and respect for one another grew with the years. It was only a few months later your mom died." Peter rambled on, "and so, there we were... two men lost in remorse not knowing where the compass of life would take us. It was during this time we both decided to throw all our mental and physical energy into our new business; and with the help of your Uncle Stephen, we developed a huge business conglomerate... Double MM.

"I would look forward to playing with you three children, as I guess it was a way for me to express a fatherly love, which had been denied me with the death of my wife and daughter."

Peter walked from the window to Jen and took her hand in his and continued, "You have been like my own daughter to me and I have expressed my feelings in a fatherly manner. I think, perhaps, this is where your dad misunderstood my love, believing it was a love I would have for a sweetheart. He did not understand when I spoke of a love for you, it was in a hypothetical sense." Peter turned once again to gaze out the window into the bright sunlight and said, "Jen, I will never love another woman. My love awaits me in heaven." Peter's eyes filled with tears and the room was quiet for a long time.

Jen broke the silence, "Uncle Peter, just before dad died he mentioned there was something going on in the company, which was worrying him and he felt insecure as to how you were going to vote at the next board meeting. He said he needed you to vote with him, but that is all he told me." In a regretful tone of voice, Jen murmured, "Dad told me if we married, he would feel our marriage would solidify a stronger union between you two."

Peter was surprised to hear this and the shock was clearly expressed on his face.

"Yes, Martin was right. There are things evolving in the corporate office from circumstances, which were inevitable to develop from decisions made years ago. Martin and I were always on the same page regarding our policies for the company; but with the continued growth and with new members on the board of directors, things are starting to happen, which have me a little concerned."

Jen wanted to explain further and said, "Uncle Peter, you can imagine how surprised I was when dad suggested the two of us marry. My feelings for you are exactly the feelings I would have for a relative... you know, I like you, but I don't love you. And I'm really sorry if I hurt your feelings the other day by the sarcastic remark I made by suggesting my dad's wife could marry you. That was really cruel, but I hope you can now understand why I said it."

Peter pulled Jen from the chair and gave her a big hug and in a soulful manner volunteered, "Jen, I will always think of you as the daughter I never had. My cherished memories of the great times you, Kat, Marty and I had when you three were growing up will remain with me always." With firm conviction, he continued, "I want you to call me any time, day or night, if you need help… after all, you have always called me uncle and I want our relationship to continue." He kissed her on the forehead and left the studio.

Jen watched Uncle Peter walk to his car with a firm steady step, shoulders pulled back stretching to his full height. He exuded an arrogant demeanor, which exemplified a powerful man who could be in complete control of any situation. His stride reminded Jen of his entrance into the study for the reading of her dad's will, and she believes, perhaps, this physical exterior façade is his defense in the business world where he must put up a tough front against all adversaries. Jen is happy he never showed this pompous attitude when visiting Mason Manor. He was always very kind and soft spoken with a mild manner just like he was this morning.

Jen took a deep sigh of relief believing the discussion was a revelation obliterating any worries she had about a possible marriage between her and Uncle Peter. She felt like the weight of the world had been lifted from her shoulders. With a smile she thought: *Uncle Peter is still a good friend and I know I will be able to count on him and Marty if I really need help… and I also have Darren.*

She walked to the front of the studio to talk to Sally, when she saw a white Chevy pick-up truck slowly drive down the street. She realizes not all of her worries have ended.

Chapter Eighteen

It was three o'clock in the morning and Eileen was still pacing the floor in her bedroom trying to decide if she should call Darren. The information she has would incriminate her to some extent, but she wants Darren to know all the facts about certain events, which may help him solve her husband's murder. With strong conviction, she dials the phone.

"Darren, it's Eileen. I hope you don't mind my calling you at this late hour, but there is something I should have told you when you were out here. It's about the jewelry."

Darren rubbed his eyes, glanced at his alarm clock on the nightstand while yawning, "Couldn't this have waited until morning?"

"No! Just listen! First, I want to make it clear that I did not take the diamond necklace that Martin accused Kathryn of taking, which she denied and accused me. I don't know what happened to the necklace... all I know is I don't have it." She paused to clear her throat and continued, "Martin did, however, give me all the jewelry from the safe in Mason Manor and asked me to keep it in the safe at the chalet. I don't know why he did not want the twins to have it, but he didn't. He bought the jewelry for their mother, and it had not been worn for many years, and I think he wanted to give it to me so I could enjoy wearing it. He gave the jewelry to me before the party on the night he was killed and asked me to take it to Aspen as quickly as possible. This is just one of many reasons I came up here to live at the chalet so quickly after the reading of the will."

Darren injected, "Well, I guess this explains why the jewelry was not mentioned in the will. He had already given it all to you. And I also guess the jewelry is worth several hundred thousand dollars."

"Oh, yes, and probably much more," Eileen advised, "which reminds me of something else I want to tell you." Her mind is racing with many vacillating thoughts: *should I or should I not tell Darren.* "Okay, I want you to know that you are the only person who knows where the real safe is located in the chalet and you already know the combination is my birth date, which I mentioned to you when you were here. I showed you the papers to read, but I did not let you see anything else in the safe. I'm telling you this because I have been having nightmares that someone is trying to kill me; and if anything should happen to me, you will be the only one who can get the valuable contents from the safe."

Darren stopped Eileen to say, "The property deeds and contracts are equally as valuable as the jewelry."

"Yes, I thought you would agree the six-hundred-acre property deed is very important to you. Your father would be very interested in having the deed." Eileen wisely stated. "Since he is mayor of Spring Grove, I am certain he has many ways of altering dates and figures on a deed if he so chooses. I think it is probably one of the many perks of the office."

Darren was very quiet listening to this analogy while thinking: *My dad will do whatever it takes to get his hands on the deed.*

Eileen's voice started to sound more relaxed rather than high-pitched and excited as the two chatted a little longer about the colder weather in the mountains. She mentioned she was starting to feel at home in the chalet and she was looking forward to the first snowfall when she could take skiing lessons.

Her voice tightened again when she told Darren she gave her neighbors, Roger and Dorothy Taylor, his phone number in case they would have to contact him for one reason or another. Eileen whispered in the phone, "Darren, I feel much better since I have talked to you. Please keep in touch."

Darren confirmed, "I will." And the two said goodnight.

The following day was one of many, which yielded no new information in solving the murder of Martin Mason. Darren was becoming frustrated as it appeared there were no new leads for him to follow. It was late in the evening when he decided to relax and watch television when the phone rang.

"Hello." Darren leisurely answered.

"Darren? This is Roger Taylor. "I have some bad news."

Darren's heart started to race and he braced himself for whatever he was about to hear.

"Eileen is dead. She was driving up the mountain on the old narrow road with all its dangerous curves when a deer became startled by the headlights and jumped into the path of her car. It broke the windshield and killed her immediately."

Darren audibly gasped a groan of disbelief

"The bloody deer was thrown down the mountainside, but the car managed to stay on the road hugging the mountain." With a puzzled thought, Roger continued, "The police said it was an accident, but I'm not so sure. I think for as bloody as the deer was there should have been more blood on the car and on Eileen. I just thought I'd pass that on to you for what it's worth. She knew this is the rutting season when the male deer are more active and I told her to be very careful on the road at night."

Darren stopped Roger with the question, "What was she doing driving on the road at night by herself?"

"She told Dorothy she was going to take skiing lessons and asked her to keep an eye on the chalet while she was gone. A few years ago, Martin Mason gave us a key to the chalet so we could watch over things when no one is staying there. I guess we feel kind of responsible for the place." In a consoling tone of voice, Roger continued, "Eileen was sure one fine lady… Dorothy and I feel real bad."

Darren did not know how to respond or what to say as he was stunned with this news. Finally, after a few moments he volunteered, "I will fly out tomorrow and I'll bring Martin's daughter Jennifer with me. If you could have the chalet open for us, I would appreciate it. I'll call you from the airport in Aspen when we arrive."

Chapter Nineteen

Jennifer wished their flight to Aspen would have been under happier circumstances. She had been looking forward to seeing Darren again, as their last lingering kiss was invading her dreams consuming the twilight hours before morning. Thinking of him was her one reprieve from the stress and anxiety from existing problems brought about by her father's murder. To be with him was to be in a safe harbor from reality.

The time aboard the plane to Aspen afforded Darren and Jennifer an opportunity to exchange pertinent information. Each one shared possible scenarios, which, hopefully, could shed some light on the multitude of existing crimes. The investigation keeps expanding in different directions and they are confused if all these isolated tragic incidents are executed by one person or by many people to satisfy self-interests.

Jen's excitement of learning about Eileen's tragic death exhausted her emotionally; and after an hour in flight discussing tragic events, she decided to rest her head on Darren's shoulder. Darren looked at her beautiful face and kissed her lips... he knew he was falling in love. Jen smiled tenderly at Darren and closed her eyes.

Darren also closed his eyes to rest, but his mind kept racing with one thought after another: he still believes Martin Mason was being black mailed, which would explain the trashing of his office as if someone were looking for something.

His second thought: maybe his dad is taking advantage of Martin's death to retrieve the property deed from Eileen, which action could throw attention to Martin's murderer and away from him.

His third thought: who and why would someone want to kill Jen?

***

The plane taxied onto the runway and the two rented a car to drive to the chalet. Darren was very careful driving on the old narrow road up the mountainside, constantly looking for deer. Roger and Dorothy were waiting for them in the driveway.

Dorothy called, "Jennifer, honey, you keep getting prettier all the time. It's been a good two years since you've been up here. What's keeping you so busy?"

"Hi, Dorothy! Well, college graduation, a new decorating business, among a lot of other things."

"Roger and I were sorry to hear about your dad's murder … and gracious me… now your stepmother was killed."

The four entered the chalet. Darren and Jennifer did not want to discuss any details or volunteer any ideas of a serious nature with the Taylors. They kept the conversation on a lighter note and after an hour the Taylors returned to their home.

Darren's first concern was to check the safe.

"Come on, Jen, I want to show you something." Darren grabbed her hand and walked down the long glassed hallway to the master suite. He stopped in the small hallway in front of the bathroom and looked at Jen. She gave him a quizzical look, shrugged her shoulders and asked, "What is it?"

Darren smiled and said, "You are standing on the safe."

"You're kidding!" She quickly jumped away.

Darren removed the patch of carpet to reveal the safe in the floor. He was nervous when he tried the combination, but it worked perfectly. He retrieved the contents giving special care to remove all the jewelry.

Jen couldn't believe her eyes. "How did you know where the safe is? I didn't even know... and you know the combination." She said in a shocked monotone voice.

"Yes, Eileen wanted me to know, because she said no one else knows where the real safe is and no one knows the combination."

"Well, she was sure right about that!" Jen was surprised and a little disappointed her dad had never told anyone else of the location of the real safe.

Darren handed the jewelry to Jen explaining her dad had given all of it to Eileen before the party of the night he was killed and told her to keep it in the chalet safe, which she did.

Jennifer looked at the beautiful jewelry and reminisced how her mother liked to show it to her and Kat, and then would explain on what occasions their dad gave each piece to her mother. It was a special treat for her and Kat to take turns trying on the necklaces and bracelets... and then her mother would carefully place each item in its own jewelry pouch. Jen fondled the jewelry carefully, envisioning the way her mother handled it.

Darren noticed Jen appeared to be looking for a special piece of jewelry and asked, "What's the matter?"

"During our last chat with dad, when he called the three of us into the temple of doom, he accused Kat of taking a diamond necklace, which she denied immediately. Dad did not mention there was another necklace missing, which was always kept in a purple velvet jewelry drawstring pouch!" Jen exclaimed.

"Are you sure?"

"Oh, yes! That necklace is the most beautiful and most expensive one with diamonds and emeralds."

Nothing was said for a few moments as Darren could see Jen was trying to remember something. "What are you thinking?" He asked.

"I saw the pouch on the kitchen counter at Mason Manor the other evening when I visited with Wally and Della at supper. I remember giving it a second glance and wondering what it was doing on the kitchen counter. When I bid them goodnight, I glanced again at the counter to look at the pouch, but it was not there. I thought it rather strange at the time, but then I shrugged it off and forgot about it."

Jen thought: *Did Kat take both necklaces? But why was the purple velvet pouch on the kitchen counter?* She feels overloaded with problems.

Darren returned all papers to the safe and the two returned to the Great Room. They sat quietly exchanging ideas where they should keep the jewelry. They agreed Peter Fletcher would assume the jewelry was given to the twins at the time their mother died. No one knew the jewelry had been given to Eileen. It was decided Jen should take the jewelry to her apartment and not tell Kat anything until after this whole mess is resolved.

***

Roger returned to the chalet to inform Jen and Darren he had called Double MM to talk to Peter Fletcher about the funeral arrangements for Eileen. He explained Peter Fletcher handled all the details with Eileen's brother, who was the only living relative, and she was to be buried in two days, which would give the brother enough time to fly to Aspen.

Roger mentioned to Jen and Darren, "Peter was curious to hear you two were up here, and I let it suffice to say Eileen had requested Darren be advised of any problems since she had hired him to investigate Martin Mason's murder." Roger nonchalantly added.

"That was a good honest answer, Roger." Darren felt no need to explain anything further and changed the subject. "I guess Peter Fletcher will see to it you will be well compensated for taking care of the chalet until all legal matters are settled."

"My wife and I have been on Double MM's payroll for quite some time."

Darren was quick to respond, "Well, then, you already know what will be expected of you."

The three strolled outside to look at the spectacular sunset with some mountain peaks sparkling with snow. It was a beautiful, pristine view and the three stood silently for a few moments, each one engrossed in deep thoughts.

Darren felt a pang of regret Eileen would never get a chance to learn how to ski. She was certainly a complicated woman to understand, but there was one redeeming virtue: she was a liberal employer, having paid him quite a bit of money in advance, which enabled him to continue working on the case.

Jennifer no longer had pleasant memories connected with the chalet. Her tortured thoughts conjured up the many times her dad and Eileen spent together in the chalet before they married.

Roger was apprehensive wondering who would inherit the chalet, as he and his wife have enjoyed the monthly compensation from Double MM for being caretakers.

Roger was surprised to learn Darren and Jennifer had made plane reservations to return on an eleven o'clock flight that evening. His last warning to them as they drove down the driveway was, "Watch for the deer!"

Chapter Twenty

It was the end to a long arduous day when Darren pulled into the driveway at Jen's apartment. The excitement of the trip to Aspen and the red-eye flight back drained them of energy. The two young lovers stood only a few moments at the door to kiss goodnight, but the warmth of their embrace will remain in their dreams until morning.

For the first time in many weeks, Jen awoke with a smile on her face as she was happy to have spent the whole day with Darren. A fantasy of thoughts conjures up a visual picture of his ruggedly handsome face and his strong athletic build, which evokes confidence with every stride of his step. She likes the safe, warm feeling she has that he can protect her under any given circumstance, which may prevail.

Jennifer was quick to dress as she wanted to stop at the bank to open a safety deposit box before going to her design studio. Darren advised it would be better to keep the jewelry in the bank rather than in her apartment until the man in the white pick-up truck is apprehended.

***

The annoying sound of the alarm clock bristled Darren's temperament, as he was in no hurry to get up after only four hours sleep. He really wanted to turn over in bed to continue the salacious dream, which he knew he could never capture in real life. These recurring dreams have been plaguing him for the last few weeks, but at least now he can put a face on the woman in his dreams. It's Jen. With a pang of responsibility urging him to get out of bed, he decided he had better get up and face the busy day he has planned.

Darren had already obtained information from Jen regarding Wally's and Della's daily routine at Mason Manor, but now it is time to run background checks on credit and financial reports. It greatly disturbed him that Jen saw a purple velvet jewelry pouch on the kitchen counter, which raises two questions: did Della steal the diamond and emerald necklace; and how did Wally pay for the acreage he recently bought in Montana.

Jen mentioned Wally had purchased some acres close to Bozeman; and after long hours surfing the internet to obtain information on property values in Montana, he was able to find the realtor who handled the sale of the property. He was surprised to learn the land was a twenty-acre horse farm purchased for three hundred thousand dollars, which was paid in cash.

Darren pushed back from the computer to digest all the information he knew about Wally and Della when the phone rang.

"Darren? It's Della. I just had an interesting phone call from our realtor in Montana who said you had called him seeking information about the piece of property we purchased. I don't know what business you have questioning our plans to move to Montana," she emphatically stated, "but I don't appreciate your poking your nose into something that is none of your business!"

Darren apologetically stated, "Della, I hope you can understand that as an investigator for Mr. Mason's murder, I have to question everything, which may lead to a motive for killing Mr. Mason."

"All you have to do is question one of the children about our loyalty and our respect for taking care of the property and house, keeping the Mason Manor estate in excellent condition. And the children know we have always loved them." Della pleaded her case.

"I think I should tell you of a certain incident, which happened the day after Mr. Mason had been killed." Della continued, "I have not told the police, because I didn't think it had anything to do with the murder." She pondered awhile longer and told her story.

"I was delivering Mrs. Mason's breakfast tray to her bedroom the day after the murder, as she always enjoyed breakfast in bed. When I opened the door, she let out a little shriek, as if I had startled her. She was sitting on the bed with jewelry pouches spread out in front of her with an expression, which looked like I had caught her with her hand in the candy jar. She told me Mr. Mason had given her all the jewelry the night before the party." Della paused to clear her throat and continued, "I, of course, knew it wasn't true, as he had always intended to give the jewelry to the twins on their thirtieth birthday. I could see Mrs. Mason became flustered and in a quick attempt to hide her frustration, she grabbed one of the pouches and gave it to me, claiming that Mr. Mason had intended to give it to me as a gift for Wally's and my years of dedicated service. I don't think she realized the pouch she handed to me contained one of the most expensive necklaces."

Darren quickly asked, "So, you sold the necklace and purchased the horse farm?"

"Wally and I discussed at great length if we should keep the necklace or give it to the twins and we decided we did not want to get involved in an ugly situation, which should be resolved between the twins and Mrs. Mason, so we said nothing and kept the necklace."

Darren asked, again, "So, you sold the necklace?"

In a self-reproaching and regretful tone, Della softly answered, "Yes, we sold the necklace to fulfill our dream of owning a horse farm."

The phone line went quiet for a few moments as both Darren and Della were in their own little world of thoughts.

Finally, Della volunteered, "Darren, I want you to know Wally and I have been good caretakers and have showered the children with love. I also want you to know Mr. Mason was generous in paying our wages, but he was a tough task master and not an easy man to like. There were no gray areas of tolerance. It was all black and white... you either did an exceptionally good job or you were out. He and Wally got into arguments many times over how to handle the horses... with cruel words being said by Mr. Mason. Wally just took it, as I guess any good employee would."

Darren questioned, "Is there anything else you want to, or should, tell me?"

Della replied, "No. I just wanted to clear up how we got all that money to purchase the property. I think we came by it in an honest way and we have no regrets in keeping the necklace and then selling it. Mrs. Mason said the jewelry had been given to her, so we accepted it as a gift."

After the phone conversation ended, Darren sat for a long time mulling over all the information regarding the necklace. He rationalizes that Mrs. Mason took the jewelry as insurance for being able to sell a piece now and then in order to maintain the chalet in Aspen, if by necessity she should need more money.

His thoughts dwell on Mrs. Mason. She was a woman who truly baffled him with her many misleading disguises of personality and character changes while hiding behind a veil of secrecy. Her life was a living sham... weaving lies to elevate her position in life.

The afternoon sun had set and the room was getting dark when Darren finally realized it was time for dinner. He shook his head with regret thinking: *Eileen was a complicated woman.*

Chapter Twenty-One

Brothers, Martin and Stephen Mason, developed the Double MM Corporation... Martin provided the wisdom and Stephen provided the seed money to start the business. No one could have conceived its growth would amass a wealth in billions of dollars. Their most whimsical purchases of companies can greatly affect the stock market, causing stock brokers to monitor their every move, carefully. Since Martin's murder, Stephen believes he alone should sit at the helm of the Double MM steering committee to determine the direction of all the companies.

Two corporate titans of Double MM, Stephen and his son Richard, sat in Martin Mason's office to talk when they did not want to be disturbed. The office has not been occupied since Martin's murder.

"I don't care what Martin and I wrote in the bylaws years ago. We were young and floundering to make our little company grow." Stephen said throwing his arms around in amazement and continued, "There is no way we could have imagined it would mushroom into this large conglomerate of widely diversified companies."

"Well, it has! And now what are we going to do about it?" Richard acknowledged. "You and Uncle Martin stipulated Marty was to be the heir apparent to succeed as co-chairman when one of you should die... and I cannot believe how you two could have done such a stupid thing!"

"Now, son, don't question our motives for something we did years ago. I didn't think there would be a chance I would ever have a son... and Martin and I wanted the company to stay in the family, believing one of us would die first." Stephen admonished.

"It was several years later your mother and I adopted you." Stephen soulfully uttered while looking tenderly at his son.

"I wonder if Marty knows the heir apparent clause exists." Richard pondered.

"I don't believe he does; but if you recall at the last board meeting, Peter suggested the bylaws should be revised to cover more adequately the growth of the company. I believe Martin was concerned the vote would go against keeping the clause, since Marty has no experience in the business." Stephen enforced his thought, "You and I definitely would have voted against Marty coming into the corporation at the top to co-chair with me;" and with a worried thought Stephen continued, "I wonder how Peter would have voted."

"Dad," Richard began, "It wasn't until after the last board meeting when I found out about the heir apparent clause, and I'm wondering why my name was not added years ago to become a successor if one of you should die?"

"Son, I had forgotten about that clause until Peter brought it to our attention at the board meeting, but I think Martin and I did alright by you when we made you the corporate chief finance officer after only three years experience in the accounting office." Stephen assured.

The answer only slightly appeased Richard. He is still concerned Marty will become co-chairman.

"What do you think of Marty working in Rome as a sales representative?" Richard questioned.

"Martin and I discussed it right before he was killed. When Peter reminded everyone at the board meeting about the heir apparent clause, Martin thought it was imperative Marty should start working for Double MM, immediately. Eventually, Martin wanted his son to become a vice president of overseas operations and we believed the district office in Rome would be the best place for him to learn the business, starting as a sales representative. It will be interesting to see how he handles the job. He's only been in Italy a couple of weeks and I've asked Massimo to send me a progress report once a month.

"I intend to follow his 'career' very closely." Stephen sarcastically answered. "I definitely do not want that goof-off sitting next to me at the table advising me, or even suggesting, how to run this business!"

"I'm sure Massimo will watch him very closely, as he has proven to be one of our best district office managers. Nothing escapes his attention." Richard affirmed.

The conversation ended abruptly when the secretary knocked on the door to alert Stephen his two o'clock appointment had arrived.

"One more thing, Richard," Stephen quickly said. "Who is the new young man in the accounting department? Can we afford him? I saw him park in the garage yesterday and he was driving a BMW M5. That car costs more than mine!" Stephen curiously inquired.

Richard did not want to divulge the real reason for hiring him. His answer was short and nonchalant, "He used to work in our Detroit office. He's a pretty sharp guy so I brought him into the corporate office. His name is Sean O'Leary."

***

Richard stormed back to his office with a heavy, quick step; asked his secretary to get Sean into his office immediately and slammed the door.

Sean is a new employee in the corporate accounting office, transferring from the Detroit district office. His appearance is unforgettable as he is very short with a heavy muscular build, a black mustache and horn-rimmed glasses.

Richard was furious! "What the hell are you doing driving an expensive car to the office. I told you to keep a low profile."

"Don't get so excited. No one knows me in this office; and with my new black hair and mustache, and horn-rimmed glasses, no one from the Detroit office could recognize me either at first glance.

Hell, I hardly recognize me when I look into the mirror!" Sean barked back with glaring eyes trying to control his Irish temper.

"That little business arrangement we worked together is over... and don't you forget what your purpose is in this office, now! I don't want to baby-sit your every move." Richard was adamant.

Without any more harsh words being said, Sean left the office.

Chapter Twenty-Two

Italy

Marty settled in quickly to the new regimen of working as a sales representative for the Double MM district office in Rome. His affable personality and polite mannerisms opened many doors to receptive customers, and he adjusted to a routine work ethic with pleasure. He liked the freedom afforded by living in Rome and the new feeling of being "his own man", and making his own decisions.

The first shipment of meth arrived at the port in Naples, Italy, where illicit trade of drugs is the biggest commodity and then is transferred to the Double MM warehouse in Rome with no problems. The two new men, who were hired to handle the shipments, worked quickly and quietly to unload the coded designated barrels where meth was hidden. No one noticed nor suspected anything unusual, as the shipment was addressed to Marty's customers.

Marty volunteered to record the documents for his customers' shipments in the ledgers in order to help ease the accounting department's workload. He explained to Massimo, the district manager, he had graduated from college with a degree in business and accounting, and he wanted to learn the complete operation of the district office. Since the accounting department was always understaffed, Massimo greatly appreciated the additional assistance.

Marty is confident that he and Jake have devised a smooth operation for shipping meth from the Ozarks in Missouri to Rome, and a failsafe system for tracking all documentation of papers, which he will handle, personally.

Jake is thoroughly enjoying northern Italy, taking advantage of all the sport activities in the mountains and on the lakes, but his enthusiasm wanes when he has to handle his portion of the business of selling meth. His driving impetus is to have fun... he definitely does not need the money, as the steady, large income from the family oil wells in Oklahoma enables him to live a luxurious lifestyle. He enjoys the excitement of the adrenalin pumping through his veins when he talks to the meth suppliers; and for this reason, he believes it is worth the danger of surveillance by drug dealers and law officials. He is young; he is good looking; and he is ready to live life to its fullest potential.

He does not have the same diligence toward work as both Marty and Carlo, but his knowledge of the mom-and-pop meth cooking labs in the Ozarks is invaluable. Jake will stay in constant contact with these mountain dwellers to make certain the proper quantity of meth is shipped to the Double MM warehouse in Rome. These suppliers change their locations frequently from one remote area to another to avoid being caught by the authorities, and it will be Jake's responsibility to track their movements and to maintain a steady flow of meth shipments.

Carlo has established a large network of street-level associates in the large cities with the help of his many friends who are well aware of the drug-trafficking industry in Italy, thereby, making it fairly easy for him to set up a web of sellers in concentrated areas where the youth frequently hang out. The potential to sell meth to the young people at a cheaper price than cocaine is enormous, as drug consumption continues to grow.

The three men were very pleased meth was swiftly accepted by the junkies as a cheap alternative to cocaine. Their operation is running smoothly and early sales proved the business could grow quickly to proportions they never could have imagined. There is one serious problem: they failed to realize the gravity of importance their little business would have on the established market for the sale of international narcotics, including heroin coming in from the Near East and Southwest Asia, which sales are managed by Italian-based foreign organized crime groups.

They expected to have some trouble from the Mafia, but the pressure put on them from so many foreign organized crime groups is staggering and Carlo and his street associates are fearful for their lives.

Chapter Twenty-Three

Italy

... three months later

Marty's apartment is small in size and dismal in decoration, which adds nothing to uplifting the three depressed metheteers' spirits. They are nestled down in comfortable chairs, sipping a third bottle of Chianti wine, but there is no celebration.

Meth sales are great and continue to grow, especially in northern Italy where there is a higher-than-average number of drug users, which their research indicated, but they did not anticipate the director of operations of Italy's anti-drug police would dramatically increase the number of drug busts.

Marty reported, "I heard the other day the Italian narcotics division has instigated a nation-wide alert for drug abuse, especially in northern cities and along the Po River, which, get this, is called the river of cocaine…and seizures of narcotics have escalated." Jake and Carlo listened attentively and Marty continued, "This does not bode well for our little business."

Carlo asserted, "Our street associates are getting nervous and no longer know who they can trust. It's bad enough the police are working undercover masquerading as junkies, but the mobsters are threatening us to move out of their territory… and they want us to move out now, or else! And we all know what 'or else' means!"

Carlo scratched his head in dismay and continued, "These guys speak so many different languages I think the whole world is selling narcotics in Italy."

Marty injected, "Jake, have you had any trouble?"

"I think so," he answered, "two nights ago when I was in Milan, I had a black van follow me all the way to Lake Como. I quickly jumped out of the car and hopped into my boat, which I dock at the wharf to take to the waterside entrance of my condo. I'm lucky there is no other way to get home other than by boat," he pondered for a moment, "or maybe the guy was just finding out where I live. Either way, it gave me a rush of anxiety and I think we are going to have to watch our back."

Carlo volunteered, "I met with a few of my street guys yesterday on the Spanish Steps. The area was crowded with tourists so I felt comfortable sitting with them for awhile to hear if they have any concerns; and from what they told me, I think we all are starting to jump at our shadows." With a nervous chuckle he said, "I'm beginning to act like the Palestinian leader Yasser Arafat: Marty, when I'm not staying in Rome overnight here in your apartment, I'm hopping from one hotel to another... never staying two nights in the same place."

The three laughed, but they realized the seriousness of their situation. It took a fourth bottle of wine to get them talking, again.

After much deliberation, Marty finally broke the silence, "Well, I don't have the personal contact as you two do with the buyers, the cops and the gangsters, so I really can't relate to your problems on the street."

There was another long period of silence as each one tried to figure out if there are solutions to their problems without their becoming embroiled in the violence, which accompanies selling narcotics. They now realize their business venture has quickly turned into an adventure, where in the beginning, they could not fathom the depth of danger involved. They are not ready to submit to using violence to keep their business afloat... violence was not in their plan to sell meth. The plan was to start a business, which would be exciting and fun, as all three did not want to sit in an office cubical all day staring at a computer. They are pleased their business acumen is sound with the organization and development being successful, but they did not anticipate the extent of violence the business would incur from so many different nationalities.

In a very low voice, Marty softly murmured, "I'm not happy with the way things are going at home. Someone is harassing Jennifer by constantly following her; the police have no leads in the murder investigation of my dad; and Jen called to inform me that our dad's wife, Eileen, had been killed accidentally in an auto accident by a deer on the road. Perhaps, these three incidents are tied together in someway... I don't know, but I believe my place is at home."

Jake and Carlo were surprised with Marty's report of his grave situation at home and sat quietly. They did not like this new feeling of being surrounded by so many problems. All three were simultaneously thinking: *where did all the fun go?*

"In the last few days, I've been doing a lot of serious thinking." Marty talked with conviction, "My place is at home, now, where I can look after Jennifer and Kathryn; possibly help with the murder investigation... and I think it is time for me to step into the corporate office of Double MM."

Marty looked at Jake's and Carlo's facial expressions to see how they received his idea. "The three of us have put in a lot of hard work establishing our little business these last few months, but with the meager profit from selling the cheap drug meth, the business is not worth the time and aggravation... and it is certainly not worth putting our lives in jeopardy." Marty suggested.

Carlo jumped up from his chair as if to give a speech, "The important thing we learned is that we could do it! In a very short time, we have developed a successful business; and it would continue to grow, if we were willing to be as vicious and cruel as our competitors. As for me, I wanted to have a little excitement and some fun, but I'm willing to close down our operation right now." Carlo rendered his opinion.

Jake chimed in to say, "I'll go along with that. I'm a fun-loving guy. I don't want to kill anybody." And with a happy, lilting voice asked, "What do you say we take a few days and drive to the great

Mont Blanc range to watch the hang-gliders jump from the cliffs. Who knows, maybe we could muster the nerve to hang-glide, too. Let's quit our business now; bum around Europe, and play at some of the gambling casinos. What do you say?"

In a determined voice, Marty answered, "I say... I think our experience in Italy has had a sobering affect on all of us. I'm ready to assume my responsibility as head of the Mason family and establish my career in the corporate office of Double MM in Spring Grove."

The three metheteers raised their glasses in a toast for the last time in respect to bid farewell to their little business. A fraternal bond was woven among the three who carved memories with their escapades in Italy, which will last their lifetime.

With tongue in cheek, Jake soulfully said, "Gee, and I was just learning how to speak Italian."

Carlo cheerfully replied, "That's great, Jake! Say something in Italian."

"Mamma mia."

The three metheteers laughed and embraced in a brotherly hug expressing their pleasure for an exciting adventure.

Chapter Twenty-Four

Spring Grove

The dimly lit dining room created a romantic atmosphere, which was perfect for the two young lovers. A flickering candle on the table throws a soft glow, illuminating Darren's masculine, handsome features and his brown eyes. His dark hair is in stark contrast to Jennifer's long golden blonde hair and blue eyes. They epitomize the perfect, beautiful couple. They have been together quite often over the last three weeks enjoying one another's company, immensely. They were seated at their favorite table in the back corner of the room of Joe's River's Bend Steakhouse, which had become their favorite restaurant. They spoke quietly while waiting for their food, which was the best in town, but that was of little consequence since what matters most to them is they are together. The steak was tender and delicious, but they hardly noticed as both took turns reporting various incidents that had occurred since the last time they had spoken.

Jen started the conversation. "The white pick-up truck followed me again for a short distance." In frustration, she continued, "I'm never able to get the license number as the driver follows at too great a distance. I devised a plan to coax the driver to get closer to my car by my accelerating to a greater speed... then slowing down quickly to turn onto another street. I thought, perhaps, I could see the driver. The plan worked. I heard the truck's brakes screech to stop. When

I looked back at a side view of the truck, I saw the driver, but I did not recognize him. I did see he has a black mustache, but I did not get the license number."

Jen paused in the story to express her thought, "It was peculiar the driver did not continue to follow me. Instead, he sped away down a side street."

Darren could easily see Jen was shaken by the experience. He grabbed her trembling hand in comfort and offered, "The next time the truck follows you, I want you to call me on my cell phone; and if I'm in the area, I will come to you as fast as I can."

A sweet smile revealed her thanks. They sat a few moments trying to remember if they know anyone who has a black mustache and drives a white pick-up truck… but no one came to mind.

Jennifer gathered her composure and mentioned, "Marty called to say he is returning from Italy in a few days and he expects to work for Double MM in the corporate office… and Kathryn called. She plans to come home from visiting friends in Utah in a few weeks."

The conversation continued through dinner and into dessert while Jennifer expressed how happy she is both Kathryn and Marty are coming home, which will provide her with a better sense of security.

They were drinking their second cup of coffee after dessert when Darren felt he should tell Jen about his conversation over the phone with Della regarding the expensive necklace. With duplicity of thought, Jen did not know what to believe: *Did Della steal the necklace since Eileen did not know one was missing; or did Eileen give the necklace to her as Della said? Either way, it would explain why the purple velvet jewelry pouch was on the kitchen counter at Mason Manor.* The two sat quietly for a few moments, while Jen digested this news not knowing what to believe.

"Darren, I guess we will never know the truth, but I do know Della has been like a surrogate mother to me, Kathryn and Marty. And if she says the necklace was given to her by Eileen, then that is what I choose to believe." Tears filled her eyes as she continued, "I do know my dad was really mean to Della and Wally on many occasions and I would always take their side of the argument. So…

I would like you to keep this conversation between the two of us and never mention the necklace again… especially to Kathryn and Marty."

Darren shook his head 'okay' in agreement.

It was late in the evening and diners were starting to leave, but the two continued to linger at the table holding hands and speaking softly. There was so much to report they regretted not being able to enjoy an evening together without discussing problems.

Joe, the restaurant owner, nodded a friendly 'hello', but decided not to interrupt them with his idle chatter. He could see by the way they looked at each other they wanted to be alone.

With wine glasses in hand, they slowly meandered outside to the veranda to enjoy the view of a new moon with its sliver of silver shining in the sky. The cool, fall breeze from the Cedar Valley River prompted them to huddle closer together while Darren slipped his arm around Jennifer as they rested against the railing.

"You know the beautiful girl who is always in my salacious dreams… and I never want to wake up?" Darren asked.

Jen coyly whispered, "Yes."

"It's you! In fact, this morning I woke up calling your name." Darren exclaimed. "Oh, Jen, I think about you all the time… day and night."

"Darren, you make me very happy." Jen could feel the warmth of blood rush to her face and she started to cry, "I'll be glad when this whole mess is over," and she pleaded, "please, find out who killed my dad so we can get on with our lives."

He gently wiped her tears and kissed her tenderly, "My first concern is who is following you in the pick-up truck? I worry about you."

There is a certain soft tenderness revealed through the eyes of deep emotions of love, which comes from the soul; and when Darren and Jennifer look at each other, their eyes reflect this love.

After one long kiss, the two lovers left the restaurant together arm in arm wondering when it will all end.

Chapter Twenty-Five

It has been quite a few weeks since Darren talked to his dad and he is not happy sitting in the mayor's office at city hall…waiting and waiting. He took his seat in one of two very low chairs in front of the mayor's desk with his long legs sprawled under the desk. There has never been a loving father-son relationship, which Darren regrets, and the constant confrontations deepen the schism between them. His thoughts dwell upon their last meeting at his apartment after he had returned from Aspen when his dad inquired about his progress of the murder investigation of Martin Mason. The information he uncovered at the chalet regarding the existence of two deeds for the same valuable property has him greatly concerned… leading to anxiety for his dad's participation in other areas of his investigation of the murder and possibly into Eileen's death.

Martin Mason's original property deed recorded the actual date of ownership of six hundred valuable acres indicating he was the sole owner before the trial; and it was not until after his dad's testimony at the trial his name appeared on the revised deed as joint owner. Darren knows his dad is anxious to retrieve the original deed, which is still in the safe at the chalet, so he can destroy it. With Martin Mason's murder, his dad will now become sole owner; and Darren knows if the original property deed should ever surface, his dad could be either blackmailed, fined or imprisoned for giving false testimony at the trial. With a slight sarcastic smile on his face,

Darren thinks: *For being the honest mayor my dad tries to portray to his constituents, this would not bode well.*

Finally, Darren's dad walked swiftly into the office, as if he were a busy man, and sat down in a very high swivel chair behind the desk. This is a political strategy the mayor incorporates, which provides a downward gaze upon his guest, giving him a feeling of power and authority, as he sits tall, resting his arms on the desk with shoulders back.

"Hello, son, it's been awhile," he said in a stern, unfriendly voice.

"Yeah, I guess it has been."

"Your mother and I miss our Thursday evening dinner talks with you, but she assures me you have been coming over to the house Thursday at noon for lunch and she really enjoys your visits. She says it's the highlight of her day. How's everything going? Are you busy?" His dad questioned.

"I'm still pursuing the investigation into Martin Mason's murder. Thank goodness, Mrs. Mason gave me a large retainer, enabling me to stay on the case. Of course, I do have two smaller cases I am working on at the same time... oh, yes, I'm keeping pretty busy." Darren answered.

"Your mother also told me you are seeing a young lady."

"Yes, I am seeing someone pretty often. That's why I haven't been coming over in the evening."

Darren hated to lie, but there was no way he wanted to sit down to talk for a length of time on a one-on-one basis with his dad. First, he has to work out in his own mind how to handle the two property deeds in the safe at the chalet. He is not certain if there is anyone else who knows about the existence of the safe and knows the combination. All these problems were racing through his mind, when his dad posed another question.

"Do I know her?"

"I think you probably have met her when you visited Mason Manor. I'm dating Jennifer Mason."

"Was she the one who was a cheerleader in high school or was she the jock?"

"She was the cheerleader; Kathryn was the jock." Darren volunteered.

"I never could tell them apart. How is she coping with her dad's murder?"

"She's going through a difficult time." Darren was very careful not to tell his dad too much. He kept his answers short and to the point.

He squirmed in his chair, making the motion to stand when his dad looked down at him with searching eyes for an answer and nonchalantly asked, "Do you think you will be going to Aspen again anytime soon?"

"I don't think so. There's nothing to investigate at the chalet."

There was an immediate change in his dad's countenance from a stiff strained facial expression of worry to a relaxed half smile. His shoulders drooped as he fell backward into the chair. "I know the Spring Grove police department is working day and night to solve Martin's murder... and I'm keeping on top of things."

Darren made no further comment regarding the investigation as he did not want to open up a conversation that could lead to another argument. They both sat quietly for a few moments staring at one another when there was a knock on the door.

"You have twenty minutes to make your doctor's appointment." The secretary advised.

The mayor acknowledged with a "thank you".

Darren questioned, "What's wrong, Dad?"

"It's nothing, son. I have been experiencing heart palpitations, lately; and I want the doctor to prescribe different medication. That's all." He answered as he placed his fingers on his wrist to monitor the heartbeats.

They continued to stare at one another with nothing more being said when Darren took the opportunity to leave. He realizes the purpose of his dad's wanting to talk to him was to question him about the necessity to return to the chalet. He had mixed emotions as he walked to the car. He is happy they did not get into an argument, and he is greatly concerned for his dad's health. He can only imagine the stress his dad is experiencing.

Chapter Twenty-Six

Stephen closed his office door at Double MM, while looking bewildered at his son and demanded, "Calm down! I can't understand you when you yell!"

Richard clenched his teeth, made a horrible face with bulging eyes and yelled, "He's coming home!"

"Who's coming home?" Stephen asked.

"Marty is leaving Italy to work here at Double MM." Richard whined in a distressed voice, "Remember him... my oldest cousin."

"That can't be!" Stephen asserted, "He's only been over there three or four months."

"Peter Fletcher just told me the news and Marty will be in this office tomorrow. Can Marty do that? I thought Uncle Martin wanted him to stay in Italy to learn the business!" Richard declared.

"If Peter said he can come back to work in this office... then he can come back. Marty has nothing to do with you, anyway!" Stephen advised.

"The hell he doesn't! He's going to be in my accounting department for a few weeks, and then he will move into Uncle Martin's office. What the hell is going on?"

Richard was adamant, stomped around the office in total frustration and flopped into a chair.

Stephen barked into the otter office for his secretary to get Peter Fletcher on the phone.

In a controlled, quiet voice, Stephen began, "Peter, hi! Richard is sitting with me in my office and he tells me Marty is coming home. I thought he was going to remain in Rome for some time to learn business procedures in our foreign offices before taking the vice-president position in Europe."

Peter explained, "Well, that was the plan before Martin was murdered, but things are different, now. According to the bylaws, Marty will assume his dad's position. Since the board meeting is not for another three months, when we were going to vote whether or not to change certain stipulations, we have to abide by the bylaws."

"Do you mean that goof-off is going to take Martin's position sitting beside me on the board?" Stephen sternly asked.

"I have nothing to say about it. Certain bylaws were drawn up long before I joined the company. Now, you know why the forth-coming board meeting is so important. I believe every board member should be fully aware of all the bylaws pertaining to the operation of Double MM." Peter emphasized.

Stephen inquired, "Does Marty know this bylaw exists?"

"I guess he does. He called from Rome to advise he is coming home to work for Double MM in the corporate office. He said his dad had always wanted him to follow in his footsteps as head of the company along with Uncle Stephen, and he feels obligated to return... so I assume he knows about the bylaw. He will be in the office tomorrow morning." Peter went on to explain, "I told him it would be to his advantage to learn about Double MM's financial situation right away before we get into the technical portion of the conglomerate... he will have a lot to learn, quickly before taking his position as co-chairman of DoubleMM." On a brighter note, he continued, "If you remember, Marty did very well in his classes in college... and Martin always said he was proud of his grades. Let's hope we see some of that knowledge blossom here at Double MM."

Stephen wanted to vent his anger, but realized it was not Peter's fault the bylaw had been adopted many years ago at the inception of the company. With a hasty good-bye, Stephen ended the phone call.

In a defeated tone of voice, Stephen murmured, "Well, Richard, it seems there is nothing we can do about it… and I trust Peter. He knows the law."

***

Richard returned to his office, sat behind his desk with his hands at his forehead as a feeling of fear swept over him. His whole body started to shake. His mind raced from one failed plan to another that he had instigated and he believed his world was crumbling. The immediate problem had to be solved, first. Sean would have to keep a very low profile in the accounting department while Marty was in the office. He closed his eyes, shaking his head from side to side in disbelief: *If I had only known about the stupid bylaw before Uncle Martin was killed, I would not be in this mess.*

Chapter Twenty-Seven

The three sat comfortably in Jennifer's condo, while Marty expounded on his trip. Jen and Darren had many questions, seeking to live vicariously Marty's tour of the historical sites in beautiful Italy. Marty was thorough in every detail pertaining to his friends, Jake and Carlo, and the fun they had vacationing together the first week of his arrival. He, absolutely, made no mention of their business venture and he intends never to broach the experience. Once the three metheteers discovered money laundering and terrorists financing were intertwined with the drug trade, they decided it was no longer fun and games to sell crystal meth. Kathryn is the only one who knows about the three metheteers and he will ask her never to discuss their business venture with anyone. He hopes it will forever remain his secret.

Marty regrets starting Kathryn on her horrific road to addiction on crystal meth. He offered it to her as a joke… never thinking she would become a user. The drug is the most potent form of speed available and she quickly fell into a downward spiral mode to destruction. He has been in constant touch with her since she has been in the rehab center in Utah and he is looking forward to her coming home next week. In their last phone conversation, Kat reported she has been clean for two months and no longer looks like a skeleton with scales and sores.

In the last few months, he feels he has grown psychologically in behavioral characteristics attributing to a more mature mental function... and he attributes this transformation to witnessing Kat's struggle with crystal meth. He no longer wanted to be a contributor to a tweaker's drug addiction, which could kill the addict, and he definitely did not want to have this on his conscience for the rest of his life.

His thoughts no longer dwell on partying and gambling to all hours of the morning. As far as he is concerned, those escapades were experiences providing pleasure in his youth. When he left Italy, he made a pledge to take charge of his own actions. It was time to assume the responsibilities of being Martin Mason's son pertaining to Double MM and Mason Manor.

Afternoon hours melted into the evening while Marty continued to speak with alacrity when describing the many beautiful sites in Italy, professing the country is definitely a tourist Mecca. He dwelled upon the beauty of the coastal villages, to the variety of landscapes, to the highest mountains in Europe. Jen and Darren were held spellbound while he painted verbal pictures when describing the Eternal City of Rome; romantic Venice; and Florence, the birthplace of the renaissance.

Jen was surprised with Marty's sober, intelligent dissertation of his travel experiences in Italy. She remembered he made good grades in school, but she never realized he could be this zealous about anything. He was known for poking fun of every situation and he never discussed anything seriously. Jen looked at Marty across the room as if seeing him for the first time. She realizes Marty's whole demeanor has changed and Jen internally verbalizes: *Marty found his manhood in Italy.*

Darren looked at his watch, declaring it was dinnertime and suggested the three eat at his and Jen's favorite restaurant, Joe's River's Bend Steakhouse. During dinner the three discussed in great detail all the events pertaining to Martin's murder, Eileen's death, and Jennifer's harrowing experience of being followed by someone in a white pick-up truck. Jen mentioned the only identifying features she noticed when she briefly saw the driver was he has a black mustache.

The three sat silently enjoying their dinner and mulling over their previous conversation when Marty suggested: "Darren, I would like you to visit me at Double MM tomorrow if you have time. I have been in the office only a few days, but there is something I would like to discuss with you."

Darren answered, "Sure. I'll be there sometime after lunch."

Marty insisted the three have dessert as he remembered this restaurant served tiramisu, which was his favorite dessert in Italy... which would bring back pleasant memories of his two buddies he left in Italy.

Chapter Twenty-Eight

Darren entered Marty's office and was surprised to see it was a large corner office overlooking a small lake on the manicured landscape surrounding the brick and stone corporate headquarters. Darren never before gave a second thought to the grandiose size of the building; but as he delves deeper into all its component companies constituting a conglomerate, he realizes the power it can wield in the business world.

With a smile and a handshake, Marty welcomed Darren and closed his office door. "Thanks for coming. Last night, I decided we should discuss some things privately without Jen."

Darren returned the smile and curiously said, "Well, you sure have a big beautiful office for being a new employee of the company."

"Pretty nice, huh?" Marty looked around the room with a big grin on his face. "This is only the beginning of some of the things I think you should know as a private investigator.

"Upon arrival on the first day in the office, Peter Fletcher, who is the corporate attorney, handed me a large book containing all the bylaws of the company, which I read completely that night… which explains why I am sitting in my dad's office. It was stipulated that I should, upon my dad's death and after my graduation from college, inherit his position at Double MM. My dad always specified I was to join the company, but I never knew it was stipulated in the bylaws."

With a puzzled look, Darren was trying to absorb what he was being told. He continued to sit quietly and listened.

"In our last family meeting in the temple of doom, I heard my dad tell Jen there was going to be an important Board of Directors meeting and he wanted Jen to marry Uncle Peter to solidify his voting with dad on a particular bylaw. I bet this is the bylaw the Board is going to vote upon at its upcoming meeting.

"I carefully read the whole book and there is no mention of Richard's inheriting his dad's position... his dad is my Uncle Stephen, which I thought was peculiar." Marty scratched the back of his head, which is a nervous tic, and continued, "Richard and I always have had a frosty relationship and I'll never discuss this with him."

Darren questioned, "Since your dad's murder, I understand your Uncle Stephen is the executor of Mason Manor. Where does that leave you with regard to your home?"

Marty was quick to respond, "Yes, that's right. It is also stated in the bylaws, if my dad dies before I am thirty, Mason Manor will be owned and operated by the corporation under Uncle Stephen... but then I will inherit the property on my thirtieth birthday." Once again, Marty scratched the back of his head. "I don't know why dad thought his children should come into their full inheritance when they reached the age of thirty." And with a puzzled comment he slowly volunteered, "Maybe dad believed the three of us will have settled down by then."

Darren asked, "Where are you living, now?"

"I'm living at home... Mason Manor," Marty assured, "but Uncle Stephen will continue to manage the property. I'll turn thirty in a few years, and, hopefully, things will get better."

Darren was quick to ask, "Will Wally and Della continue to be the caretakers?"

"No! And it really surprises me! While Jen, Kat and I were growing up, both of them treated us as if we were their children... they were great and a lot of fun. Wally taught me everything I know about horses. Nevertheless," Marty sadly reported, "Wally said he bought some property in Montana and he and Della plan to move as soon as dad's murder has been solved."

Darren was curious to ask, "Did they mention anything else regarding the murder or any situations or events, which may have happened?"

Marty was still in a daze of disbelief that Wally and Della will move shortly and only half heard the question, but quietly answered, "No."

Darren assumes nothing was said about the expensive necklace, which paid for the purchase of their land in Montana. Evidently, Marty did not consider where they got the money... and Darren did not pursue any more questions.

The late afternoon sun started to fade in intensity as it shone through the large tinted glass windows in Marty's office, but the two young men were oblivious to the passing of time as they discussed at great length Jen's stalker. Darren is still checking records in the courthouse, regarding ownership of a white Chevy pick-up truck in the area, but without the license plate number, it is almost impossible. He has also parked at a distance outside Jen's apartment and decorating studio hoping to catch the assailant, but to no avail.

With a brightness of thought, Marty mentioned, "I don't know if there is a connection, but Jen mentioned when describing the man in the truck, he has a black mustache. There is an accountant in our office who has recently transferred from Detroit and he has a black mustache. I don't know what car he drives, but you may want to check out our parking garage and watch for him when he leaves the office." Marty sat back in his chair, scratching his head and uttered, "It's just a thought."

Darren brightened with the idea. With most of the evidence destroyed accidentally at the police station, there have been very few clues to follow and he definitely plans to check out the new accountant.

***

Darren made a point of leaving the office by way of the accounting department, hoping to catch a glimpse of the employee with a black mustache and luck was with him. It was almost five o'clock in the afternoon and Darren decided to wait outside the parking garage exit to see what model car this man drives. He sat at a distance from the exit for quite some time, when his attention was drawn to an expensive BMW M5 and behind the wheel was a man with a black mustache. His first thought was: *How can an office accountant afford such an expensive automobile!* He followed the car to a poorer section of town, which is known for many rundown apartments. The driver of the BMW parked and locked his car and proceeded to walk down the street a short distance where he got behind the wheel of a white Chevy pick-up truck. Darren was thrilled with this discovery. He wanted to jump with joy, but instead he quietly contained a victory yell: *Bingo! I've got you!*

Chapter Twenty-Nine

Darren could not contain his excitement and immediately called Jen. "I hope you haven't eaten dinner, yet." He blurted out in a high-pitched voice, "I have good news!"

The excitement in Darren's voice made Jen feel happily anxious to hear what information he had uncovered and quickly responded, "I haven't eaten, yet, and I'll meet you at the Steak House."

They both pulled into the parking lot at the same time and rushed to one another. Darren picked up Jen, swung her around and after a quick kiss on the lips said, "I think I have found the mystery man with the black mustache and the truck."

They hastened inside to sit at their favorite table. Darren was precise in every detail relating to the discovery of the stalker and he plans to fly to visit the Double MM office in Detroit tomorrow morning to find out who and why this man was transferred. He realizes he will have to call the receptionist at corporate headquarters in the morning with an excuse to talk to the new accountant in order to obtain his name... but he feels this will not constitute a problem.

With a strong caveat, Darren was emphatic Jen is to remain cautious at all times, impressing upon her they only know who he is... they do not know why he is following her. In a lighter thought, Darren expresses his belief the stalker is only seeking to harass her rather than to do her harm, but for what purpose he does not know.

Jennifer looked at Darren with soft, loving eyes and a smile on the curve of her lips while imagining a secret thought: You are my knight in shining armor!

After dinner, the two drove to Jen's condo to discuss in more detail the facts they know about this whole ugly ordeal of the investigation. Many times during the conversation, the two embraced and kissed with their close bodies melting into one... with her breasts tightly held to his chest. There was a chemistry developing between the two, which only soul mates can understand. For the first time, they realized they were meant to be together, always.

Darren pulled back from a long embrace, feeling he could burst with love. He pulled a small knife and two small Band-Aids from his pocket and slowly began: "Jen, do you recall the other evening when you told me about the book you are reading... I believe it is an old classic by Alexandre Dumas titled 'The Corsican Brothers'. You mentioned the brothers are Siamese twins and you called them blood brothers. After you told me a little bit about the story, you said you wish we could be 'blood lovers'. Well, I have an idea."

He opened the small knife and proceeded to make a tiny cut on his little finger, causing the finger to bleed; then he gave the knife to Jen and asked her to do the same. Jen was not quite certain what he had in mind, but she did as he asked.

It was a quiet moment when nothing more was said as the adrenaline rippled through their bodies producing a love which is beyond description.

Darren whispered, "Jen, we will lock are little fingers together where they are cut so our blood will flow... theoretically binding us together, and say 'key locks', which will unite us as 'blood lovers'".

It will be a night they both will remember for the rest of their life as they kissed and whispered... key locks.

***

The plane was over an hour late departing the airport, but it provided additional time for Darren to continue to dwell upon thoughts of Jennifer. He tried to relive each memorable moment of last night, while playing with the small Band-Aid on his little finger.

The stewardess stopped in the aisle to ask his preference of beverage, which jolted him back to reality, reminding him it was time to concentrate on Sean O'Leary. It was easy to obtain the stalker's name from the receptionist at corporate headquarters and he hopes to have good luck in the Detroit Office.

It was a relatively short flight and he quickly hailed a cab to drive him to Double MM's subsidiary company. He figured out a plan how to get information about Sean... hopefully from the receptionist. He does not want to involve an officer of the company who could report the interview to corporate headquarters.

Fortunately, the receptionist's desk is in the front lobby... and even better, she is a young woman by herself. Darren flashed what he considers his sexy smile and asked, "Is Sean O'Leary in today? I don't have an appointment; but since I am in the area, I thought I would make a cold call."

The receptionist flirtatiously answered with a sweet smile, "Sean was transferred to corporate headquarters in Spring Grove, Missouri. I'm afraid you're several months late."

Darren acknowledged the answer with a shake of his head, saying, "When last we talked on the phone, Sean asked if I would contact him in a few months, regarding information on an assisted-living facility for a relative who is quite elderly."

The receptionist volunteered, "Oh, he probably was asking for his Aunt Lucy;" and in a slow, sad voice she added, "she passed away."

Darren thought to himself: *That lie worked nicely.* "I never met Sean, but he certainly sounds like a nice fella... you know, with his wanting to take care of old Aunt Lucy -- and all."

The receptionist quickly turned from her desk to a big bulletin board on the wall behind her. The board was covered with schedules, meeting dates, phone calls needing to be returned by various employees, and a few pictures. She called Darren's attention to a picture of all the employees taken at a Halloween party and pointed to Sean, who was dressed as Dracula.

Darren could not believe the picture of Sean and mentioned, "You would think he would want to sport a black mustache to play Dracula. It would have helped him look more diabolic."

The receptionist laughed, "It's difficult for a young guy with light brown hair to grow a black mustache. But you're right! It would have made him look more evil."

Darren followed with a question, "I guess his move to the corporate office was a step up the ladder?"

"Oh, big time! He even bought a beautiful BMW to drive to Spring Grove as he wanted to make a good impression."

Darren thought he was going to explode with happiness after talking with the receptionist. He was going to kiss her on the cheek, but a vision of Jennifer's face passed through his mind. Instead, with a rather reserved handshake, he thanked her and drove to the airport to catch an early flight to Spring Grove.

He realizes his challenge will be to uncover the purpose for Sean's changing his appearance in Spring Grove... and that may prove to be difficult.

Chapter Thirty

Richard parked his car in the garage and hurriedly rushed to his office. His face boiled red in anger. He called to his secretary to get Sean in his office, immediately. Sean took a seat in front of the desk and sat quietly fidgeting with a paperclip not knowing what to expect.

"I can't believe you are still driving the BMW to the office. I told you to park that thing somewhere in the neighborhood close to your apartment!" Richard spoke quietly with clenched teeth and a mean look in his eyes.

"Well, now," Sean glared back with clenched teeth mimicking Richard. "I'm still driving the truck to harass Jennifer Mason! Certainly, you don't think I want to park it here at the corporate office where someone may just put two-and-two together and recognize the truck?" And to continue his thought, "Who knows? Jennifer may come to the office some day to see Marty, or her Uncle Stephen, or you, and may see the truck in the garage. No! I feel safer driving my BMW to the office."

Richard continued to pace the floor, while deep in thought, and nothing was said for a few moments. "Okay, we are going to stop harassing Jennifer. We've decided we don't want you to follow her anymore." Richard advised.

"Who are we?" Sean curiously asked.

Richard hesitated to answer the question for the moment. Vacillating thoughts went through his mind: *Should I tell Sean about all the events, which have led us to the problems we are facing today, or should I keep quiet.* Before he realized what happened, his thoughts materialized into spoken words.

"All four of us, Martin, Stephen, Peter and I were well known nation-wide as the titans of industry. To garner this much power certain transactions have to be negotiated and we were well aware of all delicate, shady financial misdeeds of white-collar crime within the conglomerate... and thanks to Peter, we have been lucky the government has not conducted a full investigation." He stopped talking and with a perplexed expression as if difficult to believe, he admitted, "And that's when you got lucky. You discovered Martin was defrauding the subsidiary company in Detroit and pocketing the money in his own personal account... unbeknownst to me, my dad and Peter. In actuality, Uncle Martin was stealing from the conglomerate. You came to me with the ledger sheets, which you said were mistakenly attached to accounting records sent from Martin's office... and the rest is history. Together, we blackmailed Uncle Martin. And for that, I felt no shame, as I figured I was only taking what belonged to the company. I did not consider it as stealing from Uncle Martin.

Sean interrupted, "We sure had a good run at it for a couple of years. The money was great!"

Richard cleared his throat and continued, "It was ironic! When Martin became tired of paying off the blackmailers... or I should say you and me, he came to me with a different story about his being blackmailed and asked if I knew someone who could put an end to his problem. After a few telephone calls, I was able to come up with a name of an assassin from Europe who could handle the job."

Richard hung his head in shame and in stupidity for the plan he devised to have Martin killed instead of Sean. He believed he would be the one to step into Martin's shoes as co-chairman of the whole conglomerate with his father.

Richard pounded his fist on the desk with such force, Sean moved sideways in his chair thinking the next thrust of his fist would be for him. He bellowed, "I can't believe I never read the bylaws of the company. I actually did Marty a favor by killing his dad… now he is the co-chairman."

With a bored expression, Sean said, "Yeah, I know all that. What I don't know is why Peter Fletcher wanted me to harass Jennifer Mason."

"First, you have to understand Peter. He is a very prideful man. At the reading of the will, Jen made a snide remark about Eileen marrying Peter that was pretty spiteful and Peter stormed out of the room. Believe it or not, he wants to marry Jennifer."

Sean asked, "Is he crazy? He's probably at least twice her age!"

Richard informed Sean, "That's when you came into the picture. Peter thought if Jen felt threatened for her life, for whatever reason, she would turn to him for safety and support." In a silly, high-pitched voice, "It would be like fairyland, where the princess falls in love with her protector. Only, it didn't work. I've heard she is seeing Darren Doyle a lot these days… which I guess you know, since you have been frequently following her for these past few months."

"Yeah, and I think they are pretty tight." Sean acknowledged.

"I think Jen is a great girl and I certainly don't wish her any harm." Richard declared.

"That reminds me. Peter has not paid me for the last few weeks; and if I am not getting paid to stalk Jen anymore, I'm going to settle my account with him and get the hell out of here. That bastard still owes me for that little job I did for him in Aspen." Sean informed.

Richard was quick to respond as he sounded off in a harsh, booming voice, "I don't give a rat's ass what you and Peter have done or plan to do! That's your problem!"

"Don't get so damned testy!" Sean screamed.

Trembling with anger and excitement, Richard rushed to Sean. With one strong hand, he grabbed him by his shirt collar and pulled him out of his chair. Richard's jugular veins protruded in his neck as he stood face-to-face glaring eyeball to eyeball shouting, "Listen up, you sonuvabitch! You had better be careful! I don't need a mealy-mouthed, good-for-nothing, little pip-squeak making noises like a real man and yelling at me! If you're smart, you'll watch your step or I will kick your sorry, puny ass out of here."

Sean was seething with rage. "That's fine with me! I'm damned tired of looking like an Italian with my black hair and stupid mustache! Hell, I'm Irish!"

Richard let go of Sean and gave him a hard push back into his chair. The thrust was so violent, Sean almost spun backwards. His whole body was shaking as he sat quietly looking at Richard.

"Okay, you've shown me your Irish temper and I'll show you mine!" Richard vehemently added, "Your work here is done! Close your desk and move out! We're through!"

Chapter Thirty-One

... one week later

Marty was deeply involved in learning his newly acquired position as co-chairman of Double MM, reading all financial reports and all important documents pertaining to the company's operation... both domestic and abroad. He is overwhelmed by it's diversification into so many different areas of commerce. The more he studies the organization, the more he admires his dad and Uncle Stephen for their astute ability in pioneering new technical methods in electronic surveillance in all facets of running their operations.

He, also, becomes aware of their many manipulations of finances, and he is not too surprised to find out their electronic banking methods make it easy to launder money abroad. He is not surprised to learn Peter Fletcher is a very important cog in the wheel of deception to steer the company on its course of appearing legitimate in every aspect of operation.

He knows he must decide whether he wants to continue in the footsteps of his dad and Uncle Stephen and close his eyes to certain shady financial manipulations; or does he want to leave the company to pursue his childhood dream of building a chain of resorts throughout the world. He and Jake discussed at great length the possibility of becoming partners in a new venture as commercial developers when they became weary of selling meth. Marty will have the financial stability behind him, as will Jake, and he knows it will be more fun to travel around the world visiting their resorts in exotic locations. He really does not want to take on the responsibility of being co-chairman of Double MM and what it legally… and illegally involves.

He enjoys the respect of all employees, which is a new feeling of importance he has never experienced, but he fears the strain of sitting in an office all day, even though it is big, will crimp the lifestyle he wishes to pursue. He realizes, now, it was always his dad's desire that he join the company… it was never his desire.

As if mesmerized by the view from his office window, Marty continued to sit in the luxurious desk chair, daydreaming of an adventuresome life… which definitely does not include selling narcotics of any kind. He dwelled upon the thought of contacting Jake to ascertain if he would be willing to start the enterprise they had previously discussed. The more Marty thought about it, the more he wanted to start the business right away.

He was startled by a loud ring of the phone. With a feeling of regret, he had to jump into reality to answer the call. "Hello."

"Hello, Marty. This is Darren. I don't get it! Where's Sean O'Leary? He hasn't harassed Jen in two weeks."

"Marty responded, "I don't know. I've been cooped up in my office reading everything the staff is throwing at me and I seldom venture into the accounting department."

Darren continued to report. "I flew to Detroit to check Sean's credentials at Double MM and found out some interesting little tidbits. Since I have returned from Detroit, I can't find him. I scoped out the area around his apartment and did not see the white pick-up truck or his BMW parked anywhere in the vicinity. In the last couple of days, I made the rounds of used-car lots and I got lucky. I found the truck! I gave the dealer Sean's description of black hair, black mustache and black horn-rimmed glasses, thinking Sean would be pretty hard to forget, but the dealer said he did not recall anybody with that description on the car lot. Marty, I think he has changed his identity, again."

"What are you talking about?" Marty asked.

"The secretary in Detroit showed me a picture of Sean and he has brown hair, no mustache and no glasses, which is his real description. If that's the case, I may have a serious problem trying to locate him. For all I know, he may have flown back to Detroit, or possibly somewhere else, or maybe he changed his name."

Marty volunteered, "I'll see what I can find out for you and call you back."

With duplicity of thought, Marty is happy that Sean is no longer harassing Jen, but he is concerned Darren cannot find him. *Has Sean left Spring Grove or is he planning something else.* Marty would like this whole mystery to be solved, now! His concern is for Jen's safety.

Marty left his office to walk through the accounting department to talk to a few of the personnel while they worked at their desk. He wanted to appear as if he were trying to become acquainted with their responsibilities, thereby believing he could ask questions. He was told the new employee, Sean, had already quit. No one knew anything about him as he did not mingle with other employees; and actually, he tried to avoid everyone. He was described as a loner.

Marty stood by the water cooler in the hall for a few minutes trying to think how he could locate Sean, when Richard came out his office and walked toward him.

Marty stopped Richard with the question, "What happened to that creepy little guy with the black mustache who worked in the accounting department?"

With a puzzled expression, Richard quietly asked, "Who?"

"You know… the new guy who drove the sharp-looking BMW. He was hired a short time ago." Marty wanted to force an answer.

"Oh, him." Richard nonchalantly answered. "I heard he quit to take another job… I think in Las Vegas."

Marty called Darren immediately to report he was unable to find out anything about Sean… even the personnel department had no forwarding address. But they both thought it interesting Richard suggested knowledge of Sean's whereabouts. *How would Richard know or why would he care if Sean moved to Las Vegas.*

Darren proffered, "Let's keep an eye on Richard."

Chapter Thirty-Two

Peter Fletcher, Richard and Stephen sat in the conference room at Double MM huddled together, speaking softly. They did not include Marty in the meeting at this time, as the discussion had nothing to do with Double MM. Each one is embroiled in his own problems involving Sean O'Leary.

Richard reported his last meeting with Sean had turned into a hostile confrontation of harsh, bombastic words... ending with his demanding Sean get out of Double MM and Spring Grove. As for as he was concerned, Sean's work was done. Richard concluded with "I never want to see him again!"

Peter reported Sean visited him shortly after his discussion with Richard and demanded all accounts for jobs performed as requested be settled, immediately.

Stephen interrupted Peter, "Have you two been operating independently and have hired Sean for jobs other than what we specified awhile ago. I thought his job ended when Martin was killed... and I definitely did not like the idea of bringing him into our corporate headquarters... disguise or no disguise." Stephen stood up and paced the floor while the other two sat quietly. "If you recall, Martin came to us for the name of an assassin to kill his blackmailer Sean, whom we hired. We found an assassin from Europe and devised a plan of our own to have the assassin kill Martin instead. And if you remember, I was definitely against having my brother killed. I must have been out of my mind to allow such a thing to happen.

Then, I rationalized… well, my brother was stealing from our own company, so let's remove him and we will take what we want from the conglomerate." Stephen turned to face Peter and Richard with a question, "Do you realize we are stealing from ourselves?" Stephen became adamant, "and, now, we are murderers! When and how is this going to end?"

Peter injected, "It can end, today! With Eileen out of the picture, I will take the chalet in Aspen, which was promised to me long before Martin remarried!" In a quiet tone, he murmured, "I guess you both know I have always had a soft spot in my heart for Jennifer, but I'm going to forget marrying her. I understand she is in love with Darren Doyle." In a lighter tone he mentioned, "Isn't it ironic! He's the private investigator who is the only one seriously trying to solve Martin's murder, Eileen's death, and Jen's problem with a stalker. Mayor Doyle has the Spring Grove police department pretty much in his pocket, and we can thank him for being a loyal supporter of Double MM."

"With Marty at the helm of the conglomerate with me," Stephen informed, "I've decided to turn over Mason Manor to him right now instead of waiting for his thirtieth birthday. I want to divorce myself from the past and concentrate running Double MM, which has its own problems."

The three started to leave the room when Richard remembered, "Peter, our board meeting is next month and we were going to vote to remove the bylaw stipulating Marty will take Martin's position at Double MM. I guess the bylaw is no longer a concern. He's already taken the position."

Peter faced Richard squarely and in an authoritative voice advised, "That's right! We could invoke a bylaw stating you will take your dad's position upon his death… if that is what Stephen wants."

Stephen nonchalantly said with a touch of sarcasm, "That's fine with me. Just don't kill me to get the job!"

With a soft, good-natured laugh, the three left the conference room.

Chapter Thirty-Three

The drive on Highway 8 from Spring Grove to Mason Manor is always beautiful. Darren and Jennifer marveled at the colorful white dogwood and redbud trees complimenting the green cedar and giant oak trees on the gentle rolling slopes of the foothills to the Ozark Mountains. Along side the road, the crystal clear Cedar Valley River rippled through small rapids while the banks of the river blossomed with mayapples and small clusters of purple violets creating a pristine picture.

Except for the beautiful spring foliage, the drive was reminiscent of Darren's first and second visits to Mason Manor last fall when he was called to investigate burglaries, which culminated to Martin's murder. Darren's first visit was a simple routine investigation initiated by Mrs. Mason, which revealed nothing was stolen. The second urgent call came from Mrs. Mason informing him Martin had been killed.

His thoughts wandered to the web of events since Martin's death. Is it possible the murder merely provided succeeding crimes to evolve, giving the perpetrator or perpetrators the opportunity to hide evil deeds amid the larger crime without being exposed.

Because Darren has devoted most of his time investigating Martin's murder, his private investigating business has suffered in the last six months. He is greatly disappointed his efforts have not produced reliable evidence to substantiate his theory... was Martin being blackmailed? The two divorce cases he handled simultaneously, which consisted of surveillance of spouses, brought in enough money to sustain him; and, happily, the hours worked paled in comparison to the hours devoted to the murder investigation. Both cases at Mason Manor remain open.

Darren and Jennifer looked forward to being alone together on Sunday afternoon as they had not been able to see one another for a few days, but Marty suggested the two visit him at Mason Manor so they could discuss Darren's trip to Detroit. Darren pulled into the long driveway and noticed Wally and a young man standing a distance away from the house… down the slope by the river. Marty met them at the front door and gave Jen a big hug. Her first thought was, *he's changed since Italy…* and for the better.

Darren questioned, "Who's the little guy talking to Wally?"

"I didn't get his name. Wally said he is the son of his friend in Montana." Marty answered.

Darren could not see the stranger's face, but there was something about his short stature, which reminded him of Sean.

"I think I'll mosey on down to talk to Wally while you and Jen play catch-up." Darren suggested.

Darren approached the two men with a big grin on his face and cheerfully called, "Hey, Wally, how are you?"

With a look of surprise, Wally extended his hand for a handshake. "What brings you out here?"

"I think Jennifer misses Mason Manor," and with a bigger grin, "and you and Della! Who's your friend?"

Wally and Darren looked squarely at the young man, who looked a little squeamish. Wally stammered to reply, but the young man quickly volunteered, "I'm Sam Olney. My dad and Wally are friends."

"It's nice to meet you. Do you live around here?" Darren asked.

"No. I'm visiting from Montana and thought I would stop to say hello to Wally for my dad." Sam replied. "Well, Wally, I guess I had better get going. I have a plane to catch… and I guess our paths will never cross again."

In a loud voice, Darren called as Sam hurriedly walked up the hill to the far side of the house. "Are you flying to Montana?"

"No," was the reply, "I'm going to Las Vegas."

Darren was certain the young man was Sean… minus the black hair and mustache, which thought was verified when he watched the young man drive away in a BMW. Once again, Darren thought: *Bingo! I've got you!*

***

Della watched anxiously from the kitchen window as Wally and Darren quickly walked with long strides up the hill to the house. Her eyes continued to follow Darren as he walked around to the front porch where Marty and Jen were talking. Wally pushed the kitchen door open with such force Della thought it was going to fall off the hinges and asked, "Who was the young man? It looked like you were getting a little hot under the collar talking with him until Darren arrived."

Wally exploded, "That little sonuvabitch tried to blackmail us!"

"What!" Della roared, "We haven't done anything!"

"You know, I have always had to report to Stephen Mason the comings and goings of people visiting Mason Manor; and for what reason, I don't know. But Stephen has kept me on a weekly payroll to watch over the property, and Sam must think I work for him. According to whatever his name is… I think he said Sam Olney… he and others were blackmailing Martin Mason. He said he would implicate me as an accomplice in Martin's murder if I did not pay him two thousand a month to keep quiet. Some how that little sonuvabitch found out we bought property in Montana and he thinks I had something to do with Martin's murder.

"Sam told me Stephen Mason would call him after talking to me as to when it would be a good time to collect the money from Martin… when there would be no one at the house." Wally scratched his head in thought, "That doesn't make any sense, because he was killed when the house was filled with party guests… unless, something in the plan went wrong."

Della asked, "Did Sam say who else was involved in blackmailing Martin?"

"No, but it sounds like there were quite a few people involved and I guess he figured I was one of them; and he must think I was hired to kill Martin Mason." Wally rationalized.

Della pleaded, "Wally, let's pack our things and go to Montana, now!"

"We can't just leave. We still have another month or so to fulfill our employees' contract with Mason Manor... and Stephen knows it."

"How did you get Sam to back off his threat of blackmailing us?" Della asked.

"I told him I had nothing to do with blackmailing Martin and I definitely did not kill him. I turned things around and told him I would go to the police immediately if he ever so much as called me on the phone or talked to me again; and then Darren came down the hill to talk to us."

Della asked, "What did Darren want?"

"I'm not sure, but I guess he wanted to say, 'hi'. He couldn't have shown up at a better time." Wally responded.

The two were interrupted when they heard the sound of rubber burning on the driveway. They looked out the window to see Darren in a car speeding down the drive by himself. Jen and Marty watched as he sped away.

Chapter Thirty-Four

Darren knew he had to catch Sean before he got on the plane or he may lose him forever. With cell phone in hand, he quickly dialed Chief Zorn at the Spring Grove police station.

"Chief?" Darren called in an excited voice, "Darren Doyle here; I think I have our man in the Martin Mason murder case, but I need your help to apprehend him."

"I'm listening!" the chief responded.

"He's driving a BMW and heading for the airport at this very minute, and I need your cop on duty to grab him before he boards a plane for Las Vegas. He's about five-feet four-inches tall with brown hair. He's wearing jeans with a brown plaid shirt and a baseball cap. His name is Sean O'Leary, but he could be traveling under an alias name: Sam Olney." Darren quickly reported.

"Where are you, now?" The chief asked.

"I'm about three or four minutes behind him driving to the airport. He must be pushing the pedal hard because I don't see him ahead of me, and I am on the long flat stretch of Highway 8."

"I will call the officer I have stationed at the airport with the car model and the suspect's physical description, immediately. I'll bring another officer with me and we'll meet you at the airport."

***

The adrenaline was flowing through Darren's veins as he accelerated to a much faster speed, throwing caution to the wind. He knew the road well, remembering the dangerous curves were a little farther up ahead and wondered if Sean knew the road as well as he... since Sean followed Jennifer many times on the same stretch of road. Darren slowed down to negotiate the curves, as they were not banked properly. He heard the screech of brakes on pavement and the sound of crashing metal on trees. When he turned the series of curves, Darren saw Sean's BMW tangled in trees. Darren pulled his car off the road and cautiously approached the BMW on foot... with gun ready.

Sean had been thrown from the BMW and was lying in a blooding heap on the ground, unconscious. Darren dialed 911 for medical assistance and then placed a call to Chief Zorn.

"There is no need to go to the airport, the suspect drove off Highway 8 at the double S curves and I have called for an ambulance." Darren apprised the chief of the situation. "Why don't you meet me at the county hospital and I'll tell you all I know about the suspect."

Chief Zorn said, "Okay, and I'll send two officers to the crash scene to check out the automobile for any pertinent evidence, and I'll meet you at the hospital."

Darren knelt beside Sean to see if he were alive when he noticed Sean's eyes open. They were eyes of emptiness... not focusing, but turned inward with Sean's agonizing thoughts: This is the second time I ran off the road at the same curve, but this time at a much faster speed... I can't feel my legs. He drifted into unconsciousness.

***

Darren returned to Mason Manor on his way to the hospital, but did not take time to explain to Marty and Jen the circumstances leading to the accident.

He and Jen looked at one another with sad, longing eyes as they had expected to spend the day... alone. They tightly clasped their tiny fingers together; whispered key locks and passionately kissed good-bye. *This little ritual has become a lovers' game, which they play quite often.*

148

Chapter Thirty-Five

Peter Fletcher and Richard could not imagine why Stephen called and told them to meet him immediately at corporate headquarters on a Sunday afternoon. They both arrived before Stephen and discussed a few scenarios, but could think of nothing to substantiate an urgent meeting. Stephen stormed into the conference room with a scowl befitting a hot-tempered disposition, bellowing, "The police have Sean!"

Both men were stunned to hear the news... each one mouthing many expletives under their breath, waiting for an explanation as to how it happened. Stephen sat down at the table, shaking his head in disbelief cursing Sean with every vile word in his vocabulary. After a few moments, he managed to contain his fury to report what had been told to him.

"I just had a call from Wally with his usual Sunday report of visitors at Mason Manor. He told me about a little guy who tried to blackmail him for the murder of Martin, but Wally was able to scare him off when Darren Doyle arrived with Jennifer to visit Marty. Wally said the little guy's name is Sam Olney and he rode away in a BMW. Darren followed the car and then returned to Mason Manor after a half hour and told them the BMW went off the road at the double S curves and Sam Olney was badly injured."

Once again, Stephen shook his head in disbelieve and yelled, "We all know Sam Olney is Sean O'Leary! Can't we get rid of this nuisance? He is always going to cause us problems."

Richard asked, "Where is Sean, now?"

"He's in the county hospital with head injuries, massive internal bleeding and two broken legs." Stephen reported.

Peter was quick to respond, "We know where he is and he's not going anywhere!" In a quiet, sinister voice said, "Let's give this some thought."

***

Hospital authorities told Chief Zorn and Darren they were not allowed to see or talk to Sean because he is still unconscious and the doctors are still accessing the extent of his injuries. The chief made it quite clear he was to be advised immediately when he could see Sean.

Chief Zorn suggested Darren drive to the police station where they could talk in the privacy of his office as he wanted to be apprised of all details pertaining to Darren's investigation.

The two sat comfortably in the chief's office, sipping on hot coffee in an effort to get a boost of energy from the caffeine. It had been a long exhausting afternoon and their meeting went longer into the evening hours. Darren explained with accuracy and precision all details pertaining to his locating and discovering the identity of Sean O'Leary. He concluded with his theory that Sean blackmailed and killed Martin Mason.

Chief Zorn lit another cigarette, stood up and walked to Darren, who was seated in front of the chief's desk, placed his hand on Darren's shoulder and in a complimentary manner said, "Son, I like your style. Your detective prowess and skill have solved a difficult case, and I don't think there is reasonable doubt to believe otherwise." As an after thought, he added, "I know your father, the mayor, will be happy to hear the case is closed. I guess your father is mighty proud of you!"

Darren did not know how to accept this accolade as he knows his father never has been proud of anything he has ever done. In a humble, quiet murmur, Darren bowed his head and said, "Thank you, sir."

Chapter Thirty-Six

Yesterday was a long, exciting, but exhausting day, and Darren decided to sleep a little longer than usual. He was disappointed he and Jennifer did not spend the day alone as they had planned, but he hoped to make it up to her today. Her studio opened at eleven on Monday mornings and he planned to surprise her at her condo with donuts and coffee for breakfast about nine o'clock. He wanted to celebrate his victory of solving her dad's murder with her. He believed he could burst with the euphoric feeling of extreme happiness... he was on top of the world. There was no tree he could not pull out of the ground by its roots. He quickly showered and dressed anticipating seeing Jen before she had to go to work.

He balanced the breakfast tray and knocked on the door. The door opened and he quickly pushed his way into the hall to place the tray on the entrance table under the mirror. He grabbed Jen's hand to find her little finger, pressed her body tightly to his, whispered key locks and smothered her with kisses. After a few moments, he realized she did not respond at first with the words "key locks", but her kisses were hard and sincere. He opened his eyes, gazed into the mirror and noticed a reflection of another Jen standing behind them. Startled, he stood back and looked at the two women standing side by side. At first glance, he could not tell them apart, but then he saw the soft, loving eyes of the woman standing farther away and realized he had just kissed Kathryn.

Jennifer stood on one foot and stamped the other, "That was quite a tryst I just witnessed… Darren and a ho making out in my entry hall. Darren how could you?" She cried. "And Kat… you encouraged him!"

Darren felt his morning happiness dissolve in Jen's tears. He threw his arms around her, trying to kiss her, but she pulled away.

"Sweetheart, how was I to know Kathryn was in town?" Darren pleaded.

Jen was furious, but soulfully uttered, "I know, Kat came in from Utah late last night. I just don't like to see you kiss someone else, especially since I couldn't be with you yesterday." She placed her head on his shoulder, "I missed you so much last night… it hurt."

Darren wrapped his strong arms around Jen and repeated, "I hurt last night, too. I love you, Jen." They kissed many times, totally ignoring Kathryn.

Kat preached, "Okay, you two break it up or at least come up for air." With disgust, Kat moved toward the door and called back, "Okay, I'm out of here. I'm going to see Marty.

***

Kathryn arrived at Mason Manor, but discovered Marty had already left for Double MM. She was surprised to learn from Wally and Della there is a "new" Marty living at home, one who is diligent, dependable, and the list went on and on as she tried to understand what has happened to her fun-loving brother. Her first thought was: *Marty will receive a tremendous salary as co-chairman, along with stock options, and many benefits including Mason Manor. He will become a very wealthy man before he is thirty. That's not fair! Her second thought was: I wonder what happened to mother's jewels?* She was interrupted in her thoughts when Della offered breakfast.

"Della, this is like old times. I miss living here and talking with you and Wally. Remember how you used to play with us and all the fun we had." Kat reminisced.

There were a few quiet moments as each one conjured up the fun times of the past. Wally broke the silence, "Things never will be the same as they were. These last six months have been awful: your dad was murdered; Mrs. Mason was accidentally killed in Aspen; and someone has been stalking Jen." Wally walked to the kitchen window to view the beautiful river below the slope of the hill and lamented, "We're moving, Kat. We've bought a little spread of property in Montana where I can raise a few horses."

Kat walked to the window and stood beside Wally. She put her arms around his shoulders in a consoling manner, "Marty kept me informed of everything happening regarding the family, but he failed to mention you and Della are moving to Montana. When do you expect to move?"

"I guess it will be pretty soon, now. I think they caught your dad's murderer… at least that's what Darren told Marty when he called late last night. You'll have to ask Marty for all the details."

Wally walked out the kitchen door to be alone with his thoughts of leaving Mason Manor. Kat and Della watched as Wally walked the beautiful, manicured grounds as if he wanted to remember each blade of grass. He loved Mason Manor.

Kat took the opportunity to be alone with Della to find out what happened to her mother's jewels.

"Well, honey, I'm not certain where the jewels are, now. Mrs. Mason told me your dad gave all of them to her the night of the big party… that is, the night when your dad was murdered. I would imagine she took them with her when she moved to Aspen, and I guess they are still in the safe in the chalet."

Della noticed Kat's expression of concern and it was obvious she was upset.

"Dad said those jewels were for Jen and me when we turned thirty! I can't believe Eileen took the jewels after dad was murdered. Does Jen know about this?"

"I guess so, although she has never mentioned anything to me about it." Della volunteered and wanted to change the subject. "Are you planning to live with Jen in town or do you think you will want to stay here at Mason Manor?"

"Right now, my things are at the condo, but I will let you know later where I decide to live." Kat replied. "I think I'll drive back to town to talk to Jen. I'll call you later."

***

Kathryn knew Jen had a customer scheduled for an appointment in her design studio, and she hoped to arrive before eleven-thirty when the customer was expected. Kat bounced happily into the studio with a big grin on her face hoping Jen will have forgotten the morning episode with Darren. Jen was not happy to see Kat walk through the door and decided to settle things once and for all.

"Kat, if you ever come onto Darren again, I'll scratch out your eyes, laughing the whole time! For some dumb reason I used to let you switch identities and get by with certain things in high school, but not now! You live your life and I'll live mine… and, perhaps, we had better not live together."

"Jen, I came to apologize for this morning. I'm sorry."

The apology took Jen by surprise and she felt herself soften toward Kat. It took Jen a few moments to realize Kat was once again playing on her sympathy and she braced her shoulders to ask, "What are you really doing here?"

"I talked to Della this morning, reminiscing about our fun times, and we started talking about dad's murder, Eileen's automobile accident with a deer and a few other things when we both realized mother's jewels were not in the safe in Mason Manor. Eileen told Della some cock-and-bull story that dad gave the jewels to her the night of the big party. Della assumes the jewels are in the safe in the chalet in Aspen. I'm hoping you know where they are; if you remember, we are to inherit them when we turn thirty. I'm hoping since Eileen is dead, we will be able to get them, now."

This information was totally disconcerting as Jen had hoped Kat would not find out or even ask about the jewels until much later. Jen thought: *Kat hasn't been home twenty-four hours and she is already asking about mother's jewels.*

Jen advised, "Don't worry about the jewels. I have them and we will divide them according to value. I think we should keep this between ourselves and not involve anyone in the corporate office or Uncle Peter. Dad gave the jewels to us. Let this be our secret."

Kat was thrilled upon hearing Jen's plan to divide the jewels. She started to say something more when the front door bell rang alerting them Jen's customer had arrived for her appointment. Jen went to the front of the store to greet her customer and Kat literally skipped out the back door... happy to be home and happy she will become rich!

Chapter Thirty-Seven

Monday, two o'clock, was tee-off time at Spring Grove Country Club golf course. Stephen, Richard and Peter reserved this time once a week to play a round of nine holes after lunch where they could discuss legal and illegal business problems without being disturbed. It has become a weekly ritual, which has survived many years of corporate growth despite seemingly insurmountable problems. Martin did not like to play golf; and as it turned out, this was his biggest mistake. He was always briefly apprised of their discussions, but there were many times when important topics were not reported.

The trio of men was playing the fifth hole when a tall distinguished-looking man expensively dressed in golf attire got out of his car, which he parked alongside an old back-country road. The strong figure moved quickly with agility through a small cluster of trees to the green at the fifth hole where the trio awaited his arrival. He joined the group making it appear as a foursome.

Richard called, "Thanks for coming. You remember Mr. Mason and Mr. Fletcher."

The mystery man acknowledged with a slight nod of his head, "How can I help you?"

Richard replied, "We have another job for you. This one should be much easier than the last one. There will be minimal planning necessary to complete the order." The mystery man gave a short, cold reply, "That's good!"

The three men continued to play golf while the mystery man walked along with them. Richard outlined the job in great detail and asked, "What's your price?"

"Five thousand dollars more than last time. No one saw me on the last job as I hid in the trees, but many people in the hospital will see me in one disguise or another."

The trio could see he was working out details in his mind and no one said anything for a few moments.

The mystery man broke the silence, "I will pack clothes, and various, necessary paraphernalia in a suitcase, which I will keep in the locker room. I will disguise myself many times during the day in order to confuse the hospital staff while learning doctors', interns' and nurses' schedules in the intensive care unit. When I return the next day, I will have the necessary fake credentials to enter the hospital as an intern. And, well, you get the idea. Leave the job to me. I'll get it done within the next few days. Deal?"

Richard, Stephen and Peter looked at one another with an approving nod and Richard cheerfully said, "Done deal."

The three men watched as the mystery man disappeared in the cluster of trees.

Stephen posed the question, "What do we know about him?"

Richard replied, "Nothing much. He's from Europe. He only can be reached by cell phone. When he answers, his moniker is: mystery man."

***

After two days in intensive care, Sean O'Leary showed no signs of improvement. With severe head injuries, he has never regained consciousness; the massive internal bleeding has not been controlled; and his two legs remain broken. The doctors refuse to operate until his vital signs improve, as they fear he will die immediately on the operating table.

Meanwhile, Chief Zorn and Darren eagerly await a message from the hospital advising when they can come to talk to Sean. They are certain they have Martin's murderer, but they still would like to get a confession.

***

The mystery man was diligent in his surveillance of schedules at the nurses' station in the center of the great room where individual small rooms lined the walls with one patient per room. He took note of all hospital personnel who visited the area. His patience endured when he had to change clothes many times during the day to alter his identity. On the third day, he dressed as an intern... he was ready to make his move.

It was mid-morning when most of the attending doctors had finished their rounds of patients. There was only one doctor at the far end of the big room assisting a patient, but he did not present a problem. The mystery man looked quite impressive dressed as an intern with his stethoscope in hand and a confident stride when he entered Sean's room. Sean was hooked up to all the necessary electrical equipment to track his vital signs. He was still unconscious. The mystery man bent very low over Sean's body as if checking for any physical signs of improvement. With his two strong hands, he pressed down very hard on Sean's chest and stomach area, holding the position for quite a few moments. He could hear ribs crack and blood gushed forth from Sean's mouth. The mystery man quickly ran to the adjacent small room while Sean's electric tracking devices buzzed alerting the nurse at the station it was an emergency. Both the nurse and the doctor ran to Sean to give assistance, but it was too late. Sean was dead.

The mystery man stopped to look at Sean while the doctor and nurse removed all the life-saving equipment and prepared the body. He nodded with a sad, sympathetic expression and immediately dashed to the locker room where he stored his suitcase. He sat for a few moments on the bench after he changed into expensive street clothes, took a deep breath as if to cleanse his soul and left the hospital with a big grin, thinking: *job easily done!*

Chapter Thirty-Eight

In a high-pitched excited voice, Jen yelled over the phone, "Darren, Uncle Peter got the chalet!"

"Calm down, Jen! How do you know?" Darren asked.

"Kat had dinner with Uncle Peter last night and he told her Double MM gave the chalet to him and they are flying to Aspen Saturday and"

"What? Is Peter going to date Kat and maybe ask her to marry him since he can't have you?" Darren interrupted.

"Oh, I don't know and I don't care." Jen nonchalantly responded in an angry voice, "Uncle Peter is very rich and Kat likes money. If she does marry him, the marriage may only last until she turns thirty, when she will inherit lots of money and whatever else from dad's will. Then she could very easily just dump him." And with an added spiteful thought, "They deserve each other."

Jen continued to pursue her original thought: "Before Uncle Peter and Kat go out there, I want us to fly to Aspen to empty the safe. I don't remember the contents, but I am certain dad kept a lot of personal papers and I definitely do not want Uncle Peter to take anything."

"Let's fly out today. I'll get the tickets and call Roger to let him know we are coming." Daren hung up the phone with a smile: *I'm going to take those property deeds for my dad.*

...

Spring rains were over and, fortunately, giant cumulus clouds gracefully hung in the heavenly blue sky, creating a relaxed, smooth flight for the two lovers as they flew to Aspen. In the distance, snow-capped mountains sparkled in bright sunlight when the plane approached the airfield.

They were surprised and happy to see Roger waiting for them in the terminal. Since they intended to return to Spring Grove on the red-eye flight at midnight, they had no checked luggage, which made for a faster departure from the airport. Darren took advantage of the drive time to the chalet to apprise Roger of all details pertaining to the capture of Martin Mason's murderer. Roger had one question, which was a little difficult for Darren to answer.

Roger asked, "Do you think Eileen's narrow escape from the grizzly bear is in anyway connected to Mr. Mason's murder?"

After a few moments to consider his answer carefully, he rationalized, "I believe Sean O'Leary was going to blackmail Eileen for some reason. After Sean killed Mr. Mason, he needed a new source of revenue, and he probably figured he could dig up something whereby he could blackmail Eileen."

"What did this guy look like... the one who killed Mr. Mason?"

Darren gave him a description and immediately Roger yelled, "I don't believe it! There was some little guy with that description walking around up here awhile back and stopped at our house for directions. He said he was hiking and got lost."

Darren volunteered nothing more than, "That's interesting."

Lingering dangerous patches of ice covered small areas of road when the temperature dipped to freezing over night, and Roger devoted his full attention to driving up the mountainside to the chalet. There was no more conversation... all three realized their precarious situation on the narrow mountain road.

Darren felt certain his theory of Eileen's death was somehow tied to Mr. Mason's murder. He believes he is right on target: Martin Mason's murder, Eileen's death and Jen's episode with a stalker are somehow all connected. And the perpetrator of all three is now dead.

After they arrived at the chalet, Roger invited them to dinner at his house, stating his wife, Dorothy, was looking forward to seeing Jen, again.

Roger jokingly said, "There's nothing in the kitchen to eat, anyway. Mr. Fletcher asked us to clean everything out so he could restock the cupboards and freezer with his own food. I guess you know, he is going to take over the chalet."

They both acknowledged with a shake of the head, but said nothing.

Jen quickly accepted the dinner offer and added, "Please tell Dorothy not to spend all day in the kitchen cooking... Darren and I are easy to please." She felt the need to explain their visit to the chalet and continued, "I have a few things belonging to my dad I want to pick up... and Darren and I will see you about six o'clock."

As soon as Roger closed the door to leave, Jen grabbed Darren's hand and the two scurried down the glass-enclosed hallway to the master bedroom to find the safe. With a swift move, Darren opened the safe, pulled everything out and scattered the contents on the floor. His keen eyes spied the property deeds packaged together as he had left them. He gave a sigh of relief.

Jen rummaged through the contents rather quickly... really not knowing why some of the papers were considered important. She planned to take them home where she could study them more thoroughly at her leisure.

Darren decided it is now or never for him to ask for the property deeds, but he is greatly concerned Jen may not understand the urgency of his request. His thoughts linger on their last evening together when he realized he can never live without her, and in no way does he want to drive a wedge between their relationships. His love for Jen comes first over his dad's need for the property deeds. Many vacillating thoughts plague him as he strives for the right decision. Finally, he decided to tell Jen everything he knows about the trial involving the sale of six hundred valuable acres on the outskirts of Spring Grove. He believed his story was accurate, as he knows the facts, and asked if the deeds could be turned over to his dad, since he is now sole owner of the property.

Jen listened intently to Darren's story. "As far as I am concerned, these deeds belong to your dad. I know nothing about the law and I certainly am not going to ask Uncle Peter." Jen grabbed Darren's little finger with hers; said key locks and kissed him. "Here, you take these deeds. I trust you."

The rest of the afternoon evolved into one beautiful day as the two enjoyed being alone. Their problems had been solved and they looked forward to a grand, glorious life together. Completely relaxed while resting his head on Jen's lap, Darren thought: *I'll call dad in the morning.*

Chapter Thirty-Nine

The plane cruised at thirty thousand feet in a sky, which was star studded like sparkling diamonds in the firmament. For the first time, Darren and Jen were able to enjoy the red-eye return flight from Aspen with no serious problems interrupting their pleasant thoughts of being together. Despite the late hour, their conversation bubbled with enthusiasm for planning their future. Now, they could put behind them all concerns of the investigation, which thoughts consumed their days and nights for many months.

Darren was happy with the accolades he earned from his peers in the police department and from the citizens of Spring Grove. *The Spring Grove Herald* newspaper splashed headlines across the first page announcing the murder had been solved, along with an article reporting the story of the investigation in accurate detail and a picture of Darren Doyle. The paper acknowledged Darren's part in handling the case to a successful conclusion.

Darren was happily surprised when he received a phone call from Stephen Mason, personally thanking him for solving his brother's murder. Peter Fletcher also called to express his thanks for his diligence in pursuing Martin Mason's murderer when the police department reportedly had no viable leads to follow. It appeared the executives of Double MM were pleased one of its corporate officers could be laid at rest knowing the murderer had been apprehended and had died for his evil deed. Darren could understand the executives' desire to feel confident the right person had been charged, thereby allowing them to have a secure feeling their life would not be in jeopardy from a co-conspirator at a future time. The corporate executives were assured the case was closed.

A high, fast wave of fame swept Darren up into celebrity status in Spring Grove and he enjoyed every minute. He believes his reputation as a competent private investigator has increased ten-fold, which could guarantee him a growth of a successful business, enabling him to support a wife.

∗∗∗

It was mid-morning when Darren awoke to the song of birds chirping outside his bedroom window. For the first time in many months, his thoughts did not go directly to the murder investigation. He felt alive and took note of his environment: noticing blossoms on the apple trees, deep green foliage of oak trees, yellow daffodils by the sidewalk… and hypothetically generalized… life is good.

He showered, shaved and dressed with enthusiasm for he believed he was going to be a messenger of good tidings. After a quick breakfast, and with property deeds in hand, he was ready to drive the short distance to Spring Grove's city hall to talk to his dad. He did not feel the weight of the world on his shoulders this morning, as was the usual feeling when confronting his dad for one of their little chats, but he literally flew up the steps two at a time to the door. With a cheerful 'good morning' to the secretary, he asked to see his dad.

The mayor stood up behind his desk with a big grin on his face, exuding happiness, "Hello, son! I'm glad you called. Your mother and I are very proud of you and what you have done for the citizens of Spring Grove. I'm sure everyone feels safer Martin Mason's murderer was caught. It means one more evil person is off the streets."

Darren thought: *I should have realized dad would equate the successful investigation by his son to helping his position as mayor, since he never forgets politics. But I think I have something else, which will make him very happy.*

"Jennifer and I went to Aspen yesterday to clear out all items from her dad's safe in the chalet before Peter Fletcher takes possession of the estate." Darren continued to report, "Jen asked me to take a look at some of the papers, which I did, when I noticed two property deeds bundled together and the one deed had your name on it as co-owner of six hundred acres on the outskirts of Spring Grove along the new highway." He paused to look at his dad's expression of considerable interest with his eyes intently focused on the package he held in his hand. He decided not to mention anything about the successful outcome of the trial after his dad's testimony, whereby his name was added to the second deed. He let it suffice he would not interfere with his dad's business… whether honest or dishonest.

"Dad, I asked Jen if I could turn over the deeds to you… since her dad is dead and your name is on the one deed. We discussed it for a short time and we believe you should have these deeds."

The mayor's serious expression of concern quickly changed to a big grin on his face and his eyes danced with delight as tears formed. Reaching for the bundle of deeds with one hand, the mayor thrust his other hand on his son's shoulder.

"Son, you have no idea how happy this makes me. I was afraid they may be in the safe at Double MM; or worse, Peter Fletcher may have them."

The two stood for a few moments with a feeling of closeness neither one had ever expressed for one another. Darren thought: *Could this be the start of a good father/son relationship?*

The big smile on the mayor's face drastically changed to an expression of pain as the mayor's body crumpled to a heap on the floor at Darren's feet. The mayor pointed to his coat jacket and in a painful whisper asked, "Son, give me the bottle from inside my jacket."

Darren quickly retrieved a pill from the small bottle and gave it to his dad.

"Don't worry, son. I have these pains quite often since my last heart by-pass. The pains don't last long." In a lighter tone of voice, the mayor continued, "I guess my old heart is not used to so much happiness at one time."

The mayor closed his eyes and fell quiet in his own thoughts … not worrying about his heart, but wondering if Peter Fletcher was aware of the two deeds. The mayor knows his worries are not over… and his heart beat grew faster, as he placed his two fingers on his wrist counting the beats.

Darren continued to sit with his dad for quite awhile as this incident made him realize how important his dad is in his life… through tough times and good times… he is his dad.

The mayor saw the deep concern on Darren's face and with soft, loving eyes uttered, "Son, don't worry. I'll be fine in a few moments."

Chapter Forty

There had not been a party at Mason Manor since last fall's social event, when Martin Mason was killed, and everyone was eager to fill the house again with happiness, which would be long remembered. It was an engagement party for Jennifer and Darren.

The weather cooperated with a full moon shining brightly on a warm summer evening. The verandah was decorated with hanging flower baskets of multiple colors with small dimly lit lanterns placed in the center of round tables covered with white table linens. Marty imported his favorite wines from Italy allowing the guests to toast the couple, and he looked forward to making the first toast of the evening as head of the Mason family. There was a big white tent erected on the manicured green lawn, which served as cover for the six-piece band and the dance floor. The guest list included relatives, members of the Board of Directors and their wives of Double MM, classmates from college and high-school days as well as newly found friends. Everyone was enthusiastic and eager to have a good time.

Wally and Della knew this would be their last party at Mason Manor. Their contract as caretakers for the property had been fulfilled and they were anxious to leave for their newly purchased horse ranch in Montana to start a new life in their golden years. They were happy to take part in the festivities, which would seal their feelings for fond remembrances spanning many years of being part of the Mason family. For this special event, they were in charge of the caterers who grilled the ribs and steaks at the huge pit in the backyard by the patio where bartenders attended an open liquor bar.

Marty has definitely decided to leave Double MM, relinquishing his position as co-chairman to pursue his childhood dream. His inheritance from his dad and Double MM will more than satisfy his need for money to start a new business venture. He likes the idea he is now the head of the Mason family and will continue to maintain the Mason Manor estate in its beautiful splendor. His first order of business will be to find caretakers who will be as devoted and hardworking as Wally and Della.

Marty's friend Jake had returned to the States from Italy a few days earlier and felt quite comfortable in the rich environs of Mason Manor. He is used to having money and all it can buy, as his wealth from oil fields in Oklahoma has continued to grow and he is richer than he had ever dreamed he would be. He is eager to continue his zealous discussion with Marty in greater detail with the possibility of becoming developers of luxury resorts in exotic locations.

Marty is very receptive to Jake's idea of first traveling to certain areas of the world in order to scout out the best locations to begin their new business venture: South Pacific islands of Fiji, Tahiti; Australia, New Zealand, Falkland Islands, South Africa, Sweden, Italy, and the Arctic are a few of many to be considered. They both became mesmerized just thinking of all the fun they will have traveling to these places… for business purposes, of course.

Marty jokingly stated, "I would like this to be a prosperous business venture… where I can grow old comfortably knowing it is a sound, honest business. I don't need another adventure in business. Life is too short."

Jake quickly replied, "Look at it this way… we can travel around for a couple of years selecting where we want to build and then we will settle down and do it."

"You make it sound so easy. My problem is with the 'settling down' part; but of course, we will have to travel around to check on our properties." Marty scratched the back of his head with the thought, "How did you come to select Sweden as a good location for a luxury resort?"

With a wide grin on Jake's face and a twinkle in his eyes he responded, "Oh, man, you should have stayed longer in Europe and traveled with me when I visited Scandinavia… what beautiful countries: Norway, Sweden and Denmark. Do you know there are over sixty nude beaches in Sweden?" Jake rolled his eyes to continue, "Man! That was really an eye-opening experience!"

Both men laughed and joined the others at the table.

***

Jennifer noticed Kathryn sat next to Uncle Peter at the table and they appeared to have eyes only for each other, which bothered her, but she knew Kat had a mind of her own and it would do no good to try to talk to her. She remembered they had spent the weekend together at the chalet and she lets her mind visualize what may have happened. She rationalized: *If Kat wants to marry him, then so be it. I never could understand her. I wonder if she is going to call him "Uncle Peter"?*

Darren and Jennifer were enraptured the whole evening by overwhelming emotions of love. Their spirits were exalted to divine heights where they knew their heart and soul were merging into one mystical experience. They looked forward to their marriage anticipating living many glorious years together. Jennifer exuded a radiant glow while showing her beautiful engagement ring to the guests and Darren beamed with happiness while talking about their impending marriage. They make a perfect couple.

After dinner and after all toasts were made, the band played the first song of the evening while Jennifer and Darren slowly danced cheek to cheek to a foxtrot amid clapping and whistling by the guests encouraging the couple to kiss. Darren took Jen's little finger in his; softly whispered key locks in her ear as they looked lovingly at each other and kissed.

Fireworks burst high into the sky with cascading sparks of brilliant colors falling to the ground. It was a surprise for the couple which Marty planned initiating the festivities of the evening and the guests enthusiastically joined in the fun. It was a beautiful party.

Chapter Forty-One

Peter Fletcher burst into Martin Mason's office at Double MM to find Stephen and Richard waiting for him. It was another sequestered meeting of the three titans.

"Well, Richard," Peter asserted, "you should be happy, now. Marty has relinquished his position and you don't have to worry about his snooping around the accounting department."

Richard shook his head in acknowledgement and urgently asked, "Do we have to include Marty in the Board of Directors' meeting, which is next month?"

"No, of course not! He's out! And there is no need to take a vote on the bylaw, which instates Marty as co-chairman. I think it's best to let certain things in the bylaws lay undisturbed and not bring up anything to the other members on the board. We should forget it. I expect Marty will be trekking off to some foreign country most of the time, anyway." And with a sly overture added, "And we will keep our eyes on Mason Manor for him."

Stephen asked with a quizzical look on his face, "What's going on between you and my niece Kathryn? I thought it was very obvious at the party you two were overly interested in one another." He did not wait for an answer, but continued, "Of Martin's three children, Kathryn is the one who is more like her dad, which may be cause for some concern. She can be mean-spirited at times and likes to play the devil's advocate." Stephen looked at Peter with sharp focused eyes, "You should know how she is… you watched her grow up."

"Yes, I do know her personality; and right now, I find it intriguing." Peter took a few moments to reflect upon their trip to Aspen and volunteered, "I may be twice her age, but I think we have the same interests and drive to succeed… and I do care for her very much. Who knows? It could lead to marriage."

"Peter, what are you doing?" Stephen yelled.

"My personal life is none of your business; and if we should marry, I could control her estate… I'm only thinking of the future for Double MM." Peter answered in a harsh tone.

Richard waited a few moments for everyone to calm down before asking, "Why did you call this meeting, Peter. What do we have to discuss. I believe everything has been nicely handled and I don't know of anything, which needs our immediate attention."

Peter started to pace the floor while Stephen and Richard remained seated and began, "Do you remember the six hundred acres Martin purchased shortly before he was killed? You know… when he had to go to court in order to claim ownership and the mayor testified on his behalf. Well, I attended the property development meeting the other night and the mayor claimed he is the sole owner. That tract of property is probably the most valuable piece of land in this area and the developers want to build a big mall. I know the mayor's name is on the deed also as co-owner, but…" Peter stopped pacing to look squarely at Richard and Stephen and emphatically informed, "money to purchase the property came from Double MM! That's right! ALL the money came from Double MM. The mayor did not put up a single penny, and yet, he is claiming sole ownership. To me, it sounds like the mayor's testimony at the trial was fabricated so Martin could purchase the property." Peter stopped to reflect upon a serious thought and with tongue in cheek slowly belabored an idea, "I think… the good citizens of Spring Grove deserve an honest mayor."

The three said nothing, but digested this knowledge to benefit them… and/or Double MM.

With a haughty attitude, Peter continued, "As attorney for Double MM, I suggest we check into the legality of the property deed the mayor has in his possession. I'm certain he will not want to remember he gave false testimony at the trial and we will get him to agree the property should revert to Double MM since the corporation furnished all of the purchase money."

Stephen was quick to inject, "I understand the mayor is not very well... I think he had a heart bypass some time ago and he is experiencing quickness of breath and heart palpitations. If we push too hard, he may have another heart attack."

Peter brightened with a calculated scheme, "Yes, that's it! He may have another heart attack!"

With an air of easy unconcern, Peter nonchalantly turned to Richard and posed a question, "Richard, why don't you call the mystery man?"

About the Author

Jeannine Dahlberg honors her Swedish heritage.., respectful of the teachings of her parents and grandparents, which she believes is evident in her writings. Her knowledge of foreign travel is incorporated in her books, allowing her to be creative in detail. She is also the author of Riding the Tail of the Dragon and Candle in the Window. She was born in St. Louis, Missouri; educated at Missouri University in Columbia and Washington University in St. Louis. She lives in St. Louis, Missouri

Other Books
By
Jeannine Dahlberg

Candle in the Window

Riding the Tail of the Dragon

Printed in the United States
125072LV00004B/292-348/P